Sarah Bednarz

Catherine Clinton

Michael Hartoonian

Arthur Hernandez

Patricia L. Marshall

Mary Patricia Nickell

WE·THE PEOPLE

Work Together

HOUGHTON MIFFLIN · Boston

Atlanta · Dallas · Geneva, Illinois · Palo Alto · Princeton

AUTHORS

Sarah Bednarz
Assistant Professor
Texas A&M University
College Station, TX

Arthur Hernandez
Associate Professor
Division of Education
College of Social and Behavioral Sciences
University of Texas at San Antonio
San Antonio, TX

Catherine Clinton
W.E.B. Du Bois Institute Fellow
Harvard University
Cambridge, MA

Patricia L. Marshall
Assistant Professor
Department of Curriculum and Instruction
College of Education and Psychology
North Carolina State University
Raleigh, NC

Michael Hartoonian
Director
Carey Center
Hamline University
St. Paul, MN

Mary Patricia Nickell
Director
High School Curriculum and Instruction
Fayette County Schools
Lexington, KY

Susan Buckley General Editor

CONSULTANTS

Felix D. Almárez, Jr.
Department of History
University of Texas
San Antonio, TX

Manley A. Begay, Jr.
John F. Kennedy School of
Government
Harvard University
Cambridge, MA

William Brinner
University of California
Berkeley, CA

Phap Dam
Director of World Languages
Dallas Independent School District
Dallas, TX

Philip J. Deloria
Department of History
University of Colorado
Boulder, CO

Jorge I. Domínguez
The Center for International Affairs
Harvard University
Cambridge, MA

Kenneth Hamilton
Department of History
Southern Methodist University
Dallas, TX

Charles Haynes
Freedom Forum First Amendment
Center
Vanderbilt University
Nashville, TN

Roberta Martin
East Asian Institute
Columbia University
New York, NY

David Northrup
Department of History
Boston College
Newton, MA

Acharya Palaniswami
Editor
Hinduism Today
Kapaa, HI

Linda Reed
Department of History
Princeton University
Princeton, NJ

Ken Tanaka
Institute of Buddhist Studies
Graduate Theological Union
Berkeley, CA

Ling-chi Wang
Department of Asian American
Studies
University of California
Berkeley, CA

TEACHER REVIEWERS

Kindergarten/Grade 1: Wayne Gable, Langford Elementary, Austin Independent School District, TX • **Donna LaRoche,** Winn Brook School, Belmont Public Schools, MA • **Gerri Morris,** Hanley Elementary School, Memphis City Schools, TE • **Eddi Porter,** College Hill Elementary, Wichita School District, KA • **Jackie Day Rogers,** Emerson Elementary, Houston Independent School District, TX • **Debra Rubin,** John Moffat Elementary, Philadelphia School District, PA

Grade 2: Rebecca Kenney, Lowery Elementary School, Cypress-Fairbanks School District, TX • **Debbie Kresner,** Park Road Elementary, Pittsford Central School

District, NY • **Karen Poehlein,** Curriculum Coordinator, Buncomb County School District, NC

Grade 3: Bessie Coffer, RISD Academy, Richardson School District, TX • **Shirley Frank,** Instructional Specialist, Winston-Salem/Forsyth County Schools, NC • **Elaine Mattson,** Aloha Park Elementary, Beaverton School District, OR • **Carmen Sanchez,** Greenbrier Elementary, School District, TX • **Irma Torres,** Galindo Elementary School, Austin Independent School District, TX

Acknowledgments appear on page 190.

Printed in the U.S.A. ISBN: 0-395-76541-2

123456789-VH-02010099989796

CONTENTS

THEME 1 We Build Communities

THEME 2 We Meet Our Needs

THEME 3 We Learn Our Rules and Laws

THEME 4 We Explore Community Changes

FEATURES

WE·THE
PEOPLE

American
Voices

We work together in our
homes, in our schools, in our
neighborhoods, and in our play.

We live together in communities—
small towns, big cities, and
wide open spaces.
We share a beautiful country!

We are one nation, one community—
of many cultures, of many ages.
We care about our families,
our friends, our country, our world.

We explore changes
together in our
communities,
for today and
for all our tomorrows!

"This land is your land, this land is my land. . ."

We are the

spirit of America!

We Build

Communities

We Build Communities

Table of Contents

September

a poem by Edwina Fallis

A road like brown ribbon,
A sky that is blue,
A forest of green
With that sky peeping through.

Asters, deep purple,
A grasshopper's call,
Today it is summer,
Tomorrow is fall.

Welcome to Our Community

People in this community are having a block party. A **community** is a place where people live and work together. A community is made up of different neighborhoods. Everyone in a community follows the same rules. People in this community are having a neighborhood block party.

4

5

Play Guess Who?

With a partner, look at all the people in the picture of the community on pages 4 and 5. What would you like to be? A police officer? A bus driver?

Here's How

- Choose someone in the picture. Don't tell your partner who you chose.

- Act out what the person is doing. Use one or two simple actions.

- Ask your partner to guess who you are.

Plan a Block Party

Imagine new students have joined your class. Plan a block party to let them know all about your school community.

Here's How

- **With a partner, draw a picture of the party you might have. What will your drawing show?**

- **Write your ideas on paper.**

- **Make a sketch.**

- **Transfer your sketch onto a big piece of paper. Add details.**

Let's Explore
Map Skills

Find Your Way!

START

First Street

Main Street

Post Road

Elm Street

N
W   E
S

Map Key

fire station	
apartment	
post office	
park	
store	
house	
school	

6

Help! I need to take this food from the store to the neighborhood party. I can follow the dotted line on the map. Here are the directions.

- Go south on Post Road to the post office.
- Go east on Main Street to Elm Street.
- Go north on Elm Street to the party.

What other ways could I get to the party?

The **compass rose** shows directions on the map. The directions are North, South, East, and West.

A **map key** has symbols on it to show where places or buildings are. A map key explains what the symbols mean.

Recipe for a Community

Ingredients:

a bunch of people

a handful of neighborhoods

a stack of rules that people obey

a scoop of ideas and interests to share with other people

a heap of different ways to get from one place to another

8

Directions:

Add all the ingredients together.

Place the people on a piece of land.

Invite them to work and play together.

Share your community with everyone!

9

Serving the Community

City

Thousands of people live and work in city neighborhoods. There are hundreds of apartments and tall office buildings. In the **city,** people can visit stores, museums, theaters, and parks. Many buses, cars, and taxis make city streets very busy.

Suburb

A **suburb** is a community near
a city. A suburb is usually smaller
than a city. Some people who live
in a suburb drive or take
a train to work in the
city. Many people
in a suburb live in
houses with yards.

Small Town

A small **town** has fewer people and is smaller than a city or a suburb. Many small towns are in the country. In some small towns there is only one main street. Most of the stores and important buildings are there.

City Counts

Walking in the city,
my dad's taking me.
I'm counting and counting
the things that I see.

800
traffic lights

a sky full of
skyscrapers

20
museums

192 parks

930 buses

pigeons, pigeons, and more pigeons

12,594 fire hydrants

221,144 cars

a lot of dogs

Suburb Sets

I took a train to the suburb
and as I went through,
I counted and wrote
all these numbers for you.

3,265
lamp posts

17
school buses

2 fire stations

960
flower gardens

1 movie theater

hundreds of hoops

2 libraries

9,700 houses

Town Tallies

Going for a drive
and looking around,
here's what I counted
today in the town.

4 baseball fields

1 million trees

28 stop signs

1,830 houses

1 ice cream parlor

4 schools

1,530 mailboxes

Classroom Counts

Look around the classroom. Pick several objects that you think are interesting to count. Work in small groups to count them.

Joan
coat rack
coats ||
boots ||| |||

Chandra
lunchboxes ||| ||
baseball hats
cowboy boots ||

Pablo
rain boots
sneakers ||||
work boots

Here's How

- Decide what each member of your group will count.

- Tally your counts on a chart.

- In your group, compare tallies.

- You can also use math stacking cubes to show your totals. How do the stacks compare?

Community Collage

What words would you use to describe your community? What pictures would you draw?

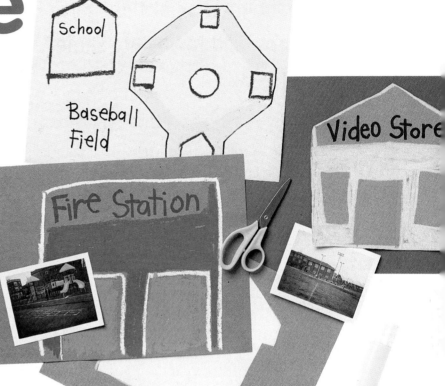

Here's How

- **Use words and pictures in a collage of your community. Glue snapshots and drawings onto a piece of oak tag.**

- **Write a description to go along with your collage.**

- **Hang your Community Collage in the classroom to share with others.**

Let's Compare

Communities share people, buildings, streets, and even rabbits. Look at the chart. How are cities, suburbs, and towns the same? How are they different?

people

City

Suburb

Town

buildings

streets

rabbits

Street Sounds

Look in your book at the pictures of a city, a suburb, and a town. What different kinds of noises might you hear in each place?

Here's How

- **Work with two or three classmates to create a "street sound symphony" for a a city, suburb, or a town.**

- **Draw a picture of something that makes a street sound.**

- **Write words on your picture that stand for the sounds you hear.**

- **Present your symphony to an audience.**

Make a Post Card!

Think about a trip to a city, suburb, or town. How would you get there? What would you see? Make a post card about your trip.

Dear Grandma,
Today we took a boat ride around the city. It was fun. Then we visited a museum I miss you!
Love, Sam

Grar
1123
Ro(

Here's How

- Draw a picture of your trip. Use the blank side of an index card.

- Turn the card over. Draw a line to divide the card into two parts.

- Write your message on the left side.

- On the right side, write the name and address of someone to whom you'd like to send your card.

Students Helping Students

What would you do if you didn't have a school to go to? Schools are important to communities. Read about how people from several communities in Maine worked together to help the students at Litchfield Central School.

Communities Reach Out

When the 150 students awoke on Thursday, March 3, 1994, they learned sad news. Their school had burned to the ground.

All the projects the students had made were gone. There were no more desks, games, or books. The fire had destroyed everything.

Volume 102   Lewiston, Maine   Friday, March 4, 1994
Journal established 1847   Sun established 1893   Sun-Journal

JACK DUGGINS photo

A fire of undetermined origin destroyed Litchfield Central School early Thursday morning. Fire officials were able to salvage a filing cabinet containing school records from the office, but books, furniture, school projects and items purchased by individual teachers with their own money were lost. An emergency town meeting will be held Saturday at 10 a.m. at Libby-Tozier School to discuss future plans, including where the roughly 150 students will attend classes for the remainder of this year.

Fire destroys Litchfield school

By KAREN MAYO
Special to the Sun-Journal
LITCHFIELD — More than 70 firefighters re-
~~~~ly morning fire Thursday

the building.
"When I got there I knew there was no stop-
ping it," he said. Labbe said his first concern
was to save the portable classrooms on the
north end of the building and a building that

cabinet from the school's office containing
records. The contents of the fire-proof cabinet
were unharmed, he said.
Two investigators from the state fire mar-
shal's office sifted through the rubble Thursday and will return to the scene Friday morn-

throughout the day.
Litchfield Central School was constructed in
1950, according to Principal Thomas Soule.
The five-classroom school and two double-wide
portable modular units, sitting on approxi-
mately four and a half acres, housed 150 of
Litchfield's elementary students in kinder-
garten through grade two, he said.
~~~ to battle the blaze

Students help to rebuild Litchfield Central School.

Soon people from other communities came to help. Portable classrooms were set up at another school. The students from Litchfield Central returned to school.

They were thankful to all who helped them.

Take Action

- Think about ways to make your school better.

- Make a list of all the ways to help.

- Talk to other people who can help you.

Tips for Helping

- Decide what you are going to do.

- Divide up the work with your classmates.

3-4-94

Hello, I

I am sorry that your school burn down☹. My school and I are sending supplies for you to use! It must be sad to have your school burn down isn't it? I hope you get a new school so you can learn more.

Sincerly,
Cory Shepherd
H.L.C Monmouth

23

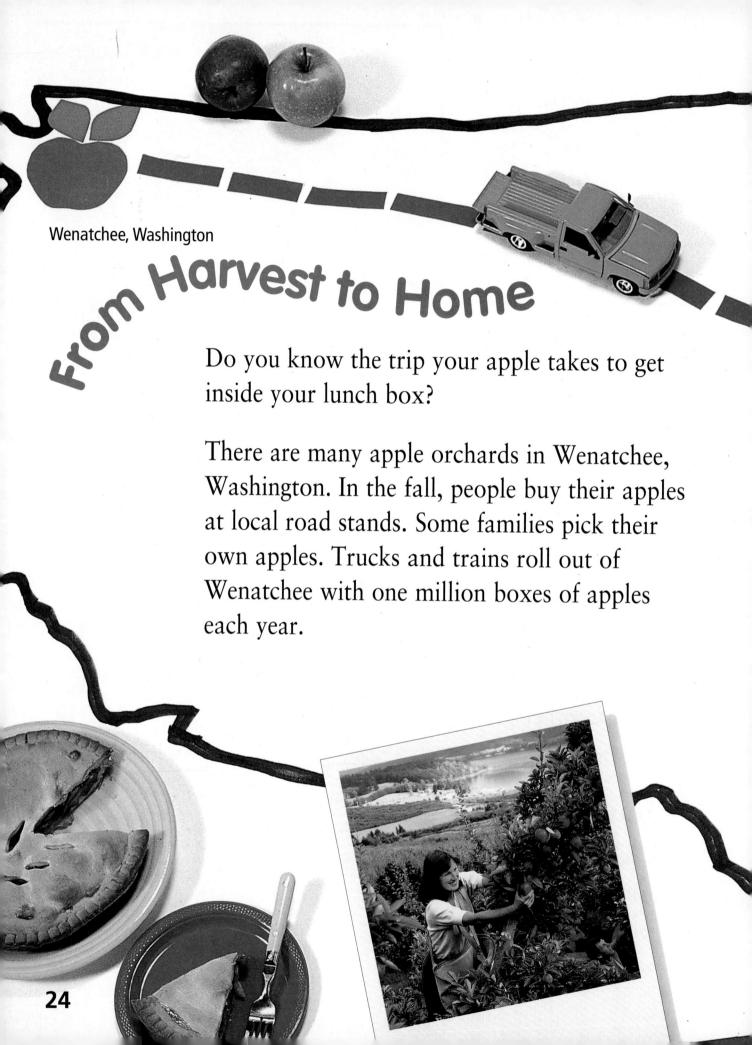

Wenatchee, Washington

From Harvest to Home

Do you know the trip your apple takes to get inside your lunch box?

There are many apple orchards in Wenatchee, Washington. In the fall, people buy their apples at local road stands. Some families pick their own apples. Trucks and trains roll out of Wenatchee with one million boxes of apples each year.

24

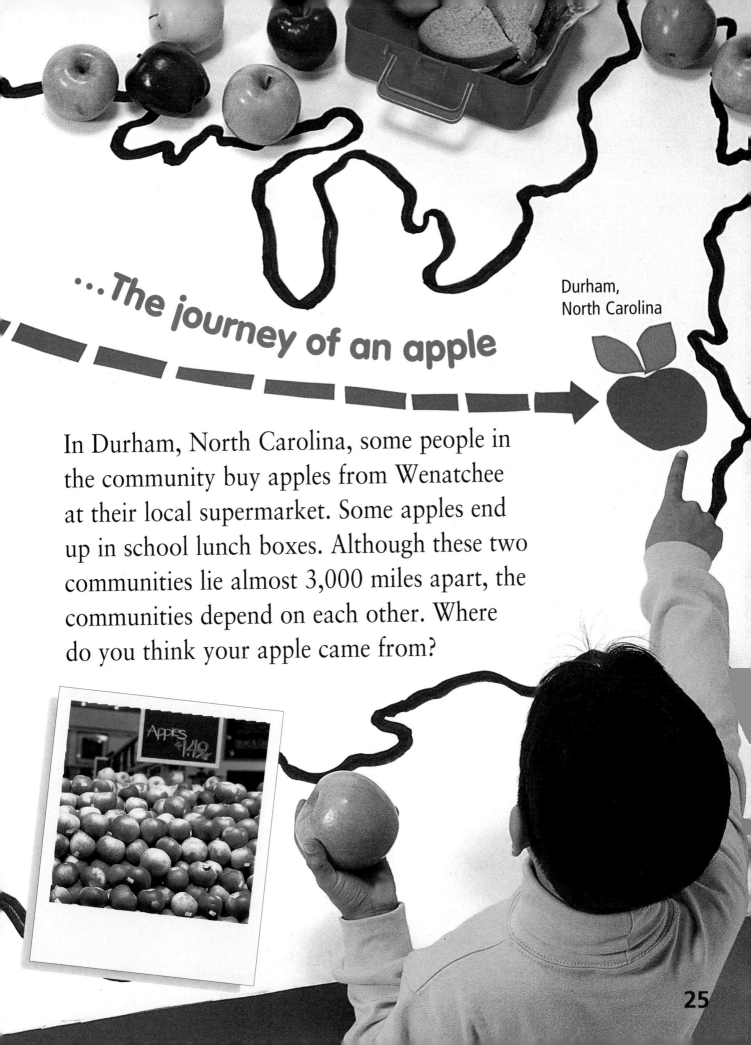

...The journey of an apple

Durham,
North Carolina

In Durham, North Carolina, some people in the community buy apples from Wenatchee at their local supermarket. Some apples end up in school lunch boxes. Although these two communities lie almost 3,000 miles apart, the communities depend on each other. Where do you think your apple came from?

Choose the Route

Imagine you are a truck driver. Your job is to get apples from Wanatchee, Washington, to Durham, North Carolina.

Here's How

- Decide which route you will take.

- Trace the route with your finger. Which direction will you travel?

- List all the states you will pass through.

- Why did you choose the route you took? Was it the shortest distance between Wanatchee and Durham?

UNI

Washington
Wanatchee
Montana
Oregon
Idaho
Wyoming
da
Utah
Colorado
Arizona
New Mexic
Alaska
Hawaii
Not to scale.

ED STATES

New Hampshire
Maine
Vermont
Massachusetts
New York
Rhode Island
Connecticut
Pennsylvania
New Jersey
Delaware
Maryland
Washington D.C.

Dakota
Minnesota
Wisconsin
Michigan
uth Dakota
Iowa
Ohio
Indiana
braska
Illinois
West Virginia
Virginia
Kansas
Missouri
Kentucky
North Carolina
Durham
Tennessee
South Carolina
Oklahoma
Arkansas
Alabama
Georgia
Mississippi
Texas
Louisiana
Florida

N
W   E
S

miles
0   200   400
0   200   400   600
kilometers

Trains

a poem by James S. Tippett

Over the mountains,
Over the plains,
Over the rivers,
Here come the trains.

Carrying passengers,
Carrying mail,
Bringing their precious loads
In without fail.

Thousands of freight cars
All rushing on
Through day and darkness,
Through dusk and dawn.

Over the mountains,
Over the plains,
Over the rivers,
Here come the trains.

Exploring the Land

People build their communities on the land and water around them. Different kinds of land are called **landforms.** Let's look at some communities.

Plains

Some plains communities have soil that is good for growing crops. There is plenty of space to raise animals.

River

River communities use fish and fresh water from the rivers. Boats carry people, food, and things made in a community to other places.

Mountain

Many people in mountain communities work on or near the land around them. People also enjoy hiking, skiing, and mountain climbing.

Island

Island communities have water all around them. Bridges, boats, and airplanes bring people and things from an island to other communities.

Community Builders

Build a different kind of community
near each landform. Be sure to show

✔ ___ a river community.
✔ ___ a plains community.
✔ ___ an island community.
✔ ___ a mountain community.

mountain

island

river

plains

33

Can You Find a Mountain?

A landform map shows the shape of the land. It can help you find landforms such as mountains, and bodies of water such as oceans.

Look at the pictures, or symbols, in the map key below. Each symbol stands for a landform or body of water. Find each symbol on the map.

Map Key

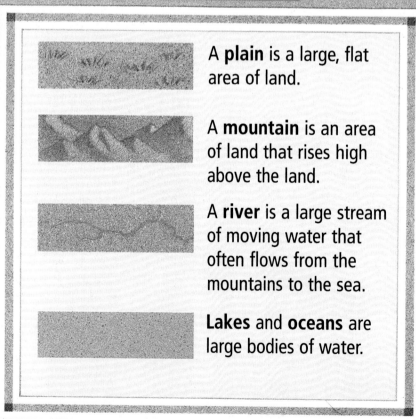

A **plain** is a large, flat area of land.

A **mountain** is an area of land that rises high above the land.

A **river** is a large stream of moving water that often flows from the mountains to the sea.

Lakes and **oceans** are large bodies of water.

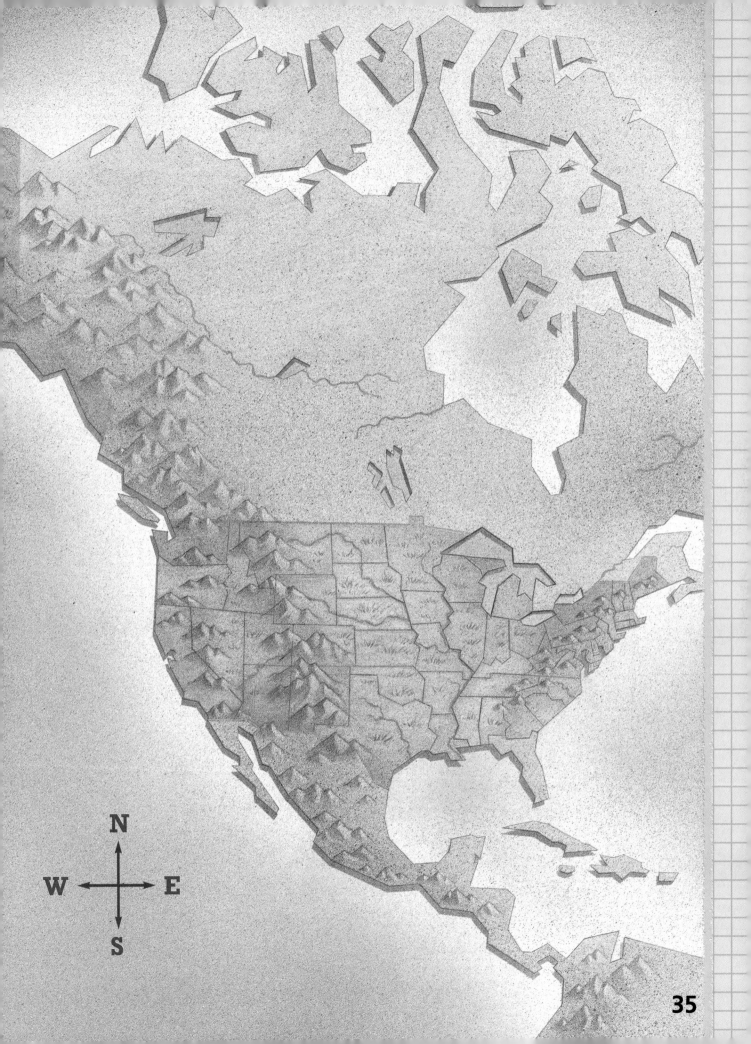

W E
N
S

Write a Poem

Use your senses to write a poem about a landform community.

mountain Community

my mountain community
smells like clean air
tastes like maple syrup
sounds like birds
feels cold
looks high

Island Community

my island community
smells like the sea
tastes like hot chocolate
sounds like a fog horn
feels sticky
looks happy

Here's How

- Write a poem about a river community, a mountain community, a plains community, or an island community.

- Copy your poem onto a piece of white paper. Add drawings to illustrate it.

- Frame your poem by gluing it onto a piece of colored paper that is a little larger than the white paper.

- Have a class poetry reading. Share your landform poetry with your classmates.

Take a Poll

Would you and your classmates like to live near a mountain or a river? On an island or a prairie? Take a poll to find out.

Here's How

- Ask your classmates where they would like to live.

- Show the results of your poll on a graph.

- Which is your classmates' favorite landform community? Which is your favorite?

A City Fights the SEA

Some communities are special because of where they are built. Galveston, Texas is on an island. People there can fish and play at beaches. However, sea waves drag away the island's sand. Large storm waves can wash right over the island.

Long ago, a hurricane made a very tall wave. It destroyed many homes and stores.

The sea wall is built of concrete and rock. It has helped protect Galveston from storms.

Galveston Island is long and narrow. It stands about seven feet above the ocean.

Galveston

What did the people of Galveston do to fight the sea? They built a sea wall to keep out waves. They also made their island higher by bringing in piles and piles of dirt and sand.

Measure 15 Feet!

The wave that hit Galveston during the hurricane was 15 feet high. Just how high is 15 feet? Use a ruler and some paper to find out.

Here's How

- Use a ruler to measure a one-foot-long strip of paper. Cut out the strip.

- Measure and cut 14 more foot-long strips.

- Tape the strips together. Try not to overlap the strips when taping them.

- Lie down next to the 15-foot strip so that your feet are at one end. Ask a friend to mark off where the top of your head is on the strip. Compare your own height to the height of the wave.

Paint a Sea Mural

Get together with a few classmates. Look through some books in your classroom or school library to find pictures of the sea.

Talk about the different ways in which the sea is shown. Then use your imagination to paint a sea mural.

Here's How

- Use watercolor paints to cover a piece of paper with color.

- When the paint is dry, add details with a dark crayon or a black marker.

- Give your sea mural a title, and hang it in your classroom.

Pittsburgh

City on a River

Pittsburgh, Pennsylvania, was built near three rivers. The rivers were full of fresh water and fish. The Iroquois people were the first to build communities by the three rivers. They caught the fish for food. As time passed, other people came to build communities near the rivers.

Look at this old map of Pittsburgh. Can you tell why part of Pittsburgh is called the Golden Triangle?

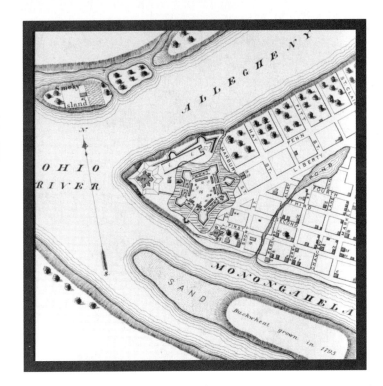

People from England built a fort by the three rivers. They named it Fort Pitt. Pittsburgh grew around Fort Pitt. People came to **trade,** or to buy and sell things. Boats carried many of the things people wanted to trade.

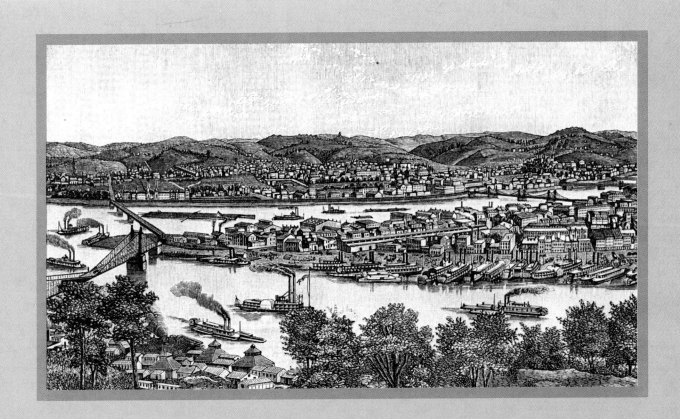

Pittsburgh became a city for making steel. Communities bought steel to build bridges, railroads, and factories. The factories made a lot of smoke. Pittsburgh became polluted.

City leaders wanted to clean up Pittsburgh. People in the community became smoke-controllers. Today, the air in Pittsburgh is much cleaner.

Why do you think Pittsburgh calls its football team "The Steelers"?

In rivers near Pittsburgh, boats still carry things to other communities.

How Did Your Town Get Its Name?

Writing a letter together is a good way for your class to get information. Use the ideas below to find out how your community got its name.

Meet with your class. Talk about what everyone wants to know. Write the questions down.

Find out who might know the answers. Get that person's address.

Work together to write your questions in a letter.

Mail your letter and wait for an answer!

42

The **date** tells when the letter was written.

September 11

Dear Ms. Torres,

The **greeting** means "hello."

Our class is doing research. We want to know how our town got its name. Do you have any information for us?

The **body** is the main part of the letter.

Yours truly,

The **closing** means "good-bye."

Room 108
Park Street School

The **name** tells who wrote the letter.

What's in a Name?

Do you know where cities, rivers, and states get their names? Some places are named for the land or water around them.

The forests in **Mesa Verde** National Park, Colorado, look flat — like table tops. In Spanish, *mesa verde* means "green table."

The **Connecticut River** is the longest river in New England. The name *Connecticut* comes from a Native American word that means "land on a long river."

Montana is known for its mountains and prairies. In fact, the word *montana* means "mountain" in Spanish.

We Meet

Our Needs

We Meet Our Needs

Table of Contents

Automobile Mechanics

a poem by Dorothy Baruch

Sometimes
   I help my dad
  Work on our automobile.
    We unscrew
    The radiator cap
      And we let some water run —
      Swish — from a hose
      Into the tank.

And then we open up the hood
And feed in oil
From a can with a long spout.
And then we take a lot of rags
And clean all about.
   We clean the top
   And the doors
   And the fenders and the wheels
   And the windows and floors....
     We work *hard*
     My dad
     And I.

Working for a Living

Many people work hard every day. There are millions of jobs to choose from. People work for different reasons. Most people work to get what they need and want.

Many people work to earn money. Money can buy the things we need and want.

Can you imagine working this high above the city?

48

A Job Toolbox

Think of a job you'd like to have. Make a toolbox and fill it with the things you would need to do this job.

Here's How

- Find a small box or other container to use as your toolbox.

- Draw pictures of tools, or cut pictures from magazines.

- You may also want to choose some "real" items to put in your toolbox.

- Share your toolbox with your classmates and parents to see if they can guess your job.

Our Needs and Wants

Needs are things people must have to live.
We all need **food** to eat. We need **clothes** to wear.
We need **shelter,** or cover, for protection.
We also need **love** and friendship. Needs are
the same for everyone all over the world.

Needs...

Wants

Wants are important too. Wants are things we would like to have. Different people have different wants. What do you want?

Persuade Your Class

Write three things you really like. Choose one thing. Now try to persuade your classmates to like the same thing!

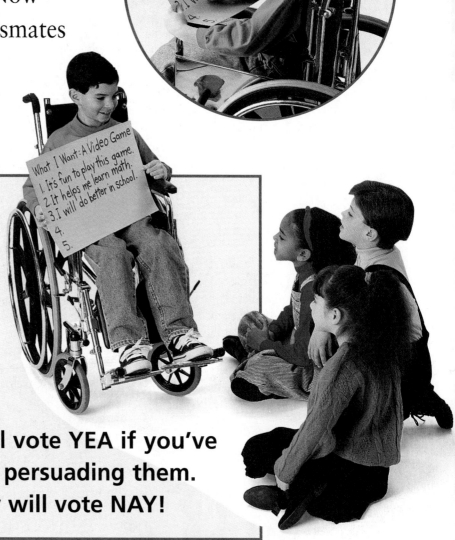

Here's How

- Do you want this thing? Write three reasons.

- Talk to your classmates. Tell them your reasons.

- Your classmates will vote YEA if you've done a good job of persuading them. If you haven't, they will vote NAY!

Needs Around the World

Work in groups to find pictures of what people around the world eat, where they live, and how they show friendship. Plan a multimedia talk with your group.

This pict...e is from Mexico. someone Tortillas pe I

Here's How

- Show a picture to the class.

- Tell what part of the world it shows.

- Explain what need is being met.

- You may want to tape-record your talk ahead of time. You can include some music, too. Then play your tape as you show your pictures.

Pilgrims

People do not always have everything they need or want. Throughout time, people have had to use things that were easy to get. People must also choose what they can afford.

In 1627, Plymouth Plantation was a village in Massachusetts where families worked hard to get what they needed. Pilgrims grew their own vegetables, milked their goats, and hunted for meat and fish.

Plantation

In Plymouth today, people have an easier time finding food, clothing, and shelter. People still grow vegetables. They can also buy food in supermarkets or go to a restaurant.

People in Plymouth worked hard and didn't always have time to make their own clothes. They had to wait for ships from England to bring cloth or clothing.

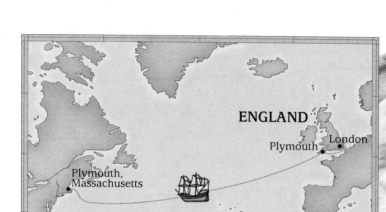

Today clothes are made in the United States as well as in other countries. Factories, machines, and computers help make clothing.

At Plymoth Plantation, men and boys built shelters from wood. They cut trees and sawed them into planks. Tall grasses called thatch reeds were found by the seashore to make roofs.

Today houses are made from materials like cement, wood, and stone. People use electric tools and machines to build shelters.

A Plymouth Plantation Skit

Imagine you lived on Plymouth Plantation
in 1627. How would you spend each day?
What would you do to make sure that you
and your family had everything you needed?

Here's How

- Visit your school library to learn more about Plymouth.

- In a group of three or four, plan a short skit that shows the different jobs family members might have had at Plymouth Plantation.

- Share the skit with your classmates.

Family Trees

Family members work on the farm.

The Greene family works on a tree farm in Grain Valley, Missouri. They plant and harvest trees. Mrs. Greene says, "Everyone in the family knows how to work every job on the farm. We work as a team to grow the best trees. Trees are a natural resource that we need to protect. A natural resource is something from nature that is useful to people."

Producers grow or make things to sell to people. The Greene family sells many things. People who buy the trees, decorations, and other products are called **consumers**.

Aaron, Lori's cousin, plows between the rows of trees.

Grain Valley

Mrs. Greene prunes trees with Garfield.

Lori started helping on the farm when she was young. She says, "My favorite job is selling trees to all the people. I also like to help my grandmother serve hot chocolate."

Lori, age ten, is selling products made on the farm.

Lori gets an allowance for helping on the farm. She spends part of it and puts the rest of it in the bank as savings. Lori says, "Last year, my brother Nick and I bought a trampoline. This year I'm saving for a bicycle."

Mr. Greene shakes dead needles from the trees.

Find the tree farm.

Adopt a Tree!

Here's How

- Take a walk around your school yard. Pick out a tree you'd like to take care of.

- Draw a picture of your tree.

- Find out more about your tree. How old is it? Talk to people who have worked at your school for a long time. Ask them how the tree has changed over the years.

- Keep a journal about your tree. Tell how it changes from one season to the next.

Nature Rubbings

- Cover your desk with newspaper. Place some leaves on the newspaper.

- Place a piece of drawing paper on top of the leaves. Hold a crayon sideways and rub it over the leaves.

- Experiment with different patterns by rearranging the leaves or by adding wildflowers. Try using different color crayons.

THE TREE

a poem by Marge Kennedy

Deep in the forest,
there stood a tall tree.
It had grown many years,
far away from the sea.
A hardworking logger chopped
the tree down.
And he took the big tree to a mill
in the town.

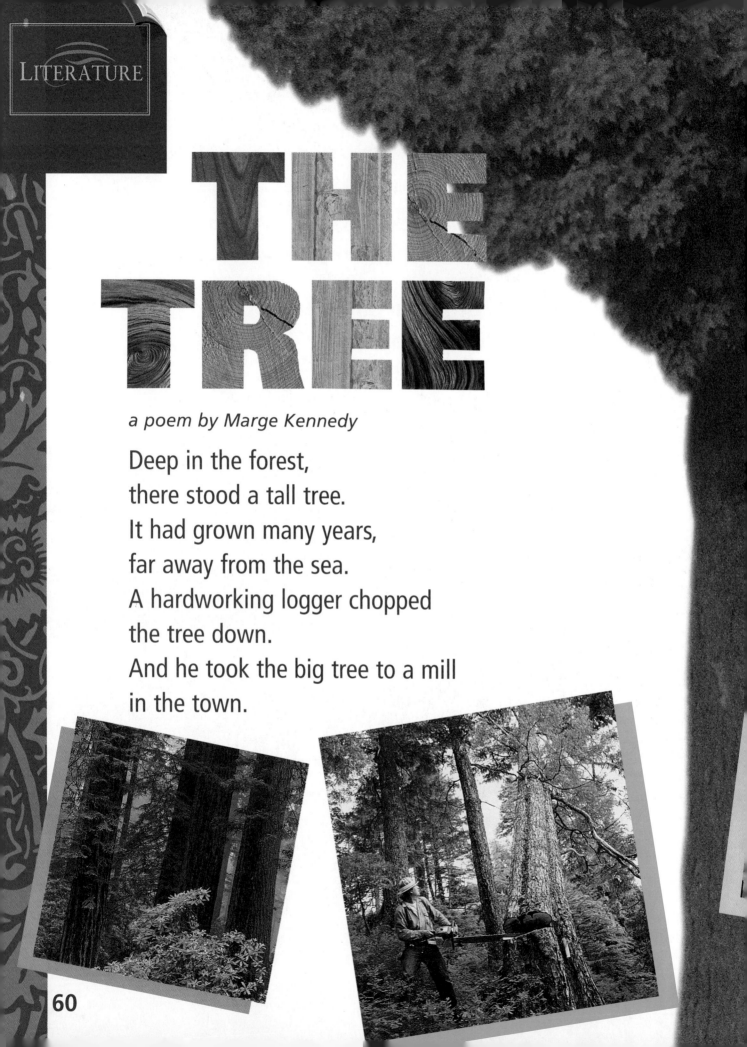

The mill stood alongside steep river banks.
A lumberjack cut the big tree into planks.
Some very wide planks were made into doors,
And some other planks became wooden floors.

61

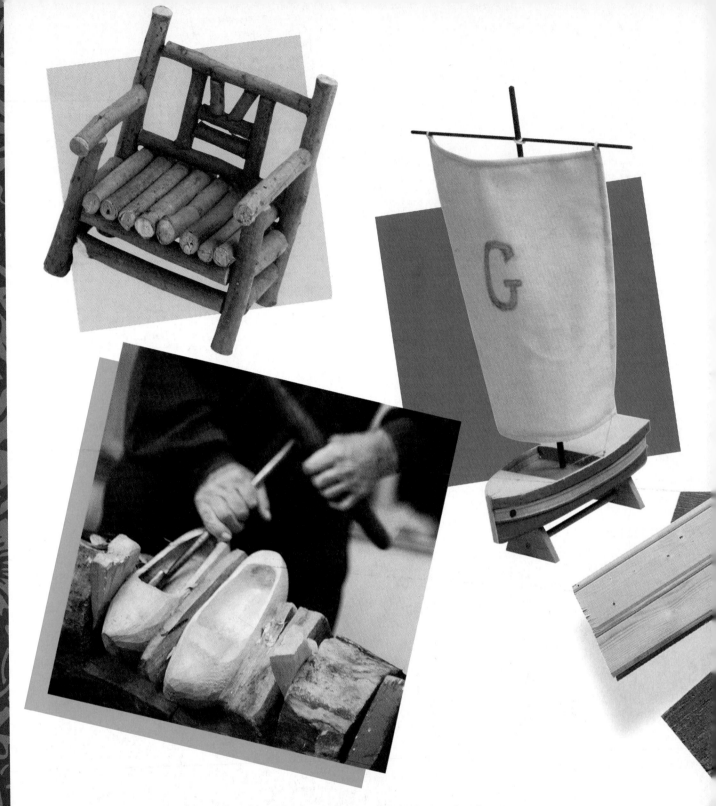

A carpenter fashioned a table and chairs.
A shoemaker carved wooden shoes — seven pairs.
And to help a sailor sail straight and sail fast,
A boat builder built a fine tiller and mast.

One sturdy tree cut with patience and care
Had helped a whole town and all who lived there.
The leftover wood became kindling for winter.
Nothing was wasted, not even a splinter.

Making a Baseball Bat

This is a **flow chart**, a type of picture that shows how something happens. The title tells you what the flow chart is about.

Start at the first box. Follow the arrows to see the order that things happen.

1 An ash tree is cut down.

2 The tree is cut into smaller pieces.

4 The finished bats are packed into boxes and sent to stores.

3 The baseball bat is shaped on a special machine.

65

From All Over!

Some wool for sweaters
comes from Peru.

Steel in ice-skate blades
might come from Brazil.

Cotton from the United
States can be made into
pants like these.

What are you wearing? Where did it come from? Maybe your shoes came from a nearby store. Where do stores get the things they sell?

Workers in factories make things called **goods** to sell. Goods are things that are made and then sold in stores.

Factories make some products from **natural resources** such as plants and things from the earth. When a factory doesn't have the materials it needs, it may buy them from other countries. People send products and natural resources all over the world by airplane, ship, train, and truck.

Asking for Answers

You can get information by talking to a person in an interview. Before you can direct an interview you must know whom you will talk to and what you want to talk about. Here are some questions you might ask if you wanted to interview someone about work.

1. What is your job? What do you do?

2. Where do you work?

3. How did you learn to do your job?

4. What do you like best about your job?

5. Do you work alone or with other people?

6 What clothes do you wear when you work?

7. What machines or tools do you use for your job?

8.. Are you a volunteer or do you get paid for your work?

ess

Just Ask!

Many workers help a community. Some are called community service workers. A service is something you do for another person. Their work helps everyone in the community.

Have you ever met the people who take care of the water that goes down your drain?

Q: Where do you work?

A: I work on water pipes underground. We make sure the pipes are clean and the water flows right.

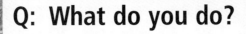

Q: What do you do?

A: I'm a foreman. My job is to make sure everything is done safely.

Q: Where does your income, or the money you make, come from?

A: People who live in the community pay **taxes**. A tax is money people pay to the government. My income is paid by people's taxes. Taxes also buy safety equipment.

Surprises

traffic guard

window dresser

sewer worker in manhole

sewer line

subway operator

Betz's

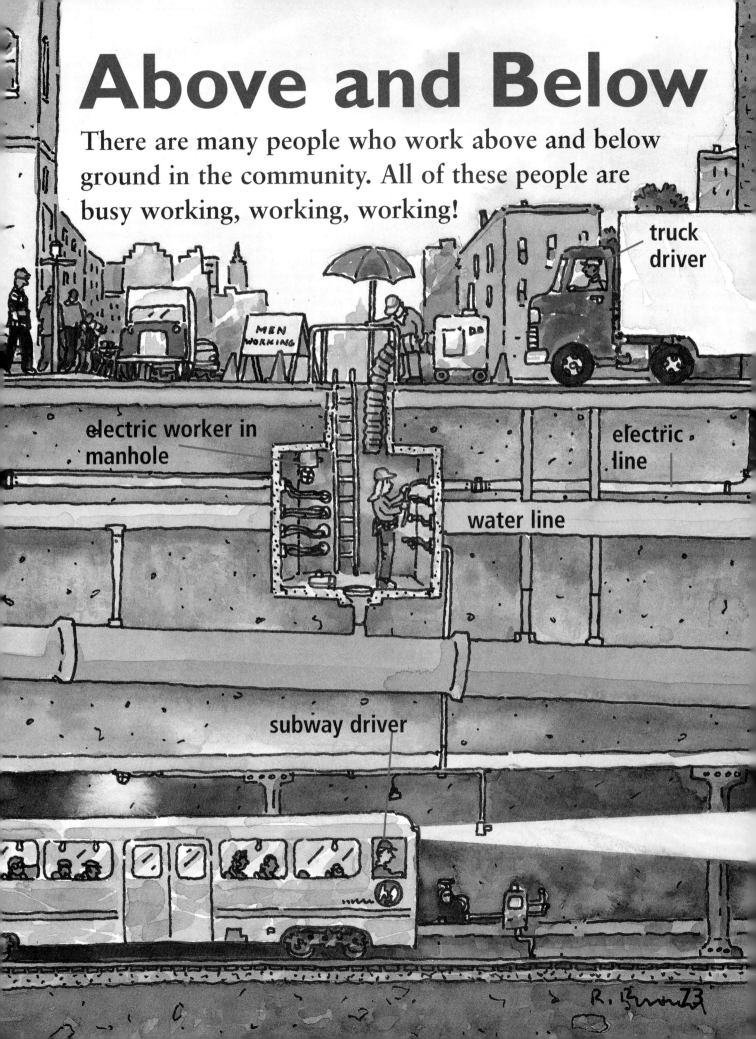

Above and Below

There are many people who work above and below ground in the community. All of these people are busy working, working, working!

truck driver

electric worker in manhole

electric line

water line

subway driver

MEN WORKING

Follow the Subway

The map on the next page shows the subway routes in part of New York City.

The letters or numbers tell the names of the subway routes, or lines. The squares show where the trains stops.

Hop on the "C" train. Take it to the Museum of Natural History.

Here's How

- Find where the "C" train starts. Follow this subway route to the museum, which is at 81st Street, right across from Central Park.

- How many stops does your train make?

- What body of water does it pass under?

- What other train could you take to get to the museum?

A Subway Map
of New York City

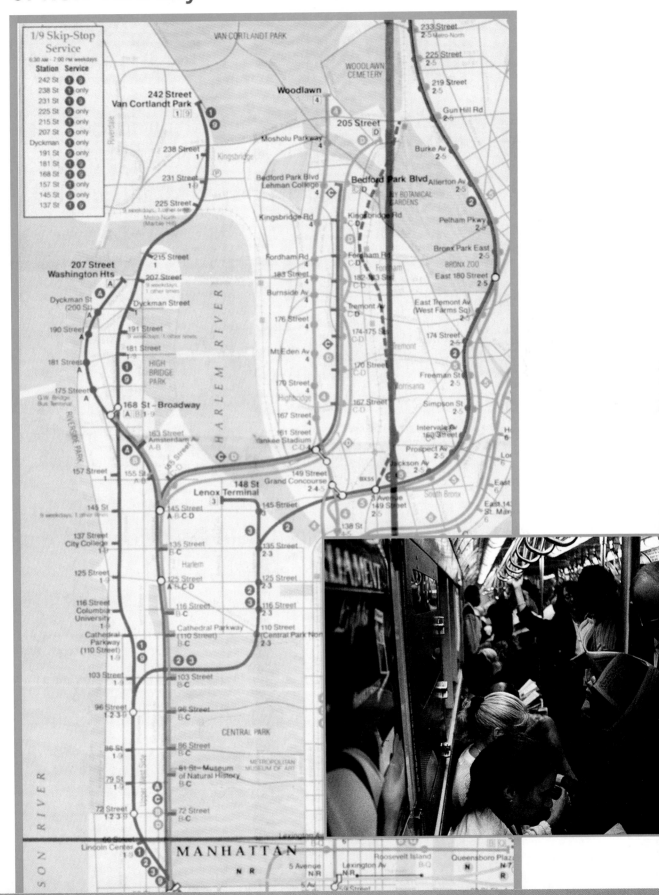

Neighbors Helping Neighbors

This is Megan, age seven. She lives in Massachusetts.

Have you ever helped a neighbor? Here is how a group called *Habitat for Humanity* helped Megan and her family build a home.

★ Volunteers Build Homes

The people who work for *Habitat for Humanity* are called **volunteers**. Volunteers are people who work for free to help others. The volunteers who built Megan's house were teachers, builders, police officers, and students. Megan says, "I helped, too. I put siding on our house and painted my closet."

Take Action

- Think of a volunteer job you could do.
- Make a list of all the ways to help.

Volunteers work hard
to finish the house.

Here is Megan and her
family outside their home.

Tips For Volunteering

- Decide what you want to do.
- Ask an adult how you can help.

Helping Hands Tree

How many ways can you think of to help others? Try filling your class with helping hands.

Here's How

- Trace your hand on a piece of oak tag. Cut it out. Make several hand cutouts.

- On each cutout, write down or draw a picture of a way in which you can help others.

- Put all the classroom hands together, and hang them on a Helping Hands Tree.

clean up bookshelves

recycle

Limpid los libreros

Make a Graph

Here's a fun way to keep track of the times you help others.

Here's How

- Find a big can or jar. Decorate the outside of the can. You may want to write the words "We Can Help" on it.

- Put the can in a special place. Store some counters. You can use paper clips or small shapes cut from paper.

- Every time you help another person, put a counter in the can. At the end of the day, count the number of counters in the can. Chart the results on a bar graph.

NATIONAL GEOGRAPHIC
world

ANTARCTICA:
CONTINENT
AT RISK

Sweet Jobs: **KIDS IN BUSINESS!**

Getting a jump on careers, from the left, teenagers Anthony Brooks, Quan Hines, and William Brooks learn how to run a business. They work at Champ Cookies & Things in Washington, D.C.

Nice Arrangement

Brandon Bosek is a budding businessman. Brandon has been running Bloomin' Express, his flower delivery service, for more than a year. "I sell flower arrangements the way other people sell magazines — by subscription," explains Brandon, 11, of Miami, Florida. "I like telling my customers about the flowers and then delivering them."

Brandon claims that Bloomin' Express flowers last longer than arrangements from supermarkets. "They're fresher," he explains.

Each week Brandon finds out what his nine subscribers want, phones in the orders to the supplier, and — with his father's help — makes deliveries.

Sometimes Brandon's mother lends a hand, too. "My mom is great about helping me figure taxes and keep records - things I haven't learned to do yet," Brandon says.

Making Dough With Cookies

Whether it's making cookies or making change, Tardkeith McBride and Maurice Cobb learn how to handle dough at Champ Cookies & Things in Washington, D.C. Tardkeith, 14, on the left, and Maurice, 15, are among more than 65 young people who operate the factory.

Ali Khan, a former teacher and school guidance counselor, started Champ Cookies four years ago with three friends. Their idea was to help keep youngsters out of the crime and drug world. "We teach them how a business runs and encourage them to take pride in their work," Khan says.

Working for a few hours after school each day, the students learn every step of the business.

In Business With Birds

Nikky Hoyne will never get caught with all her eggs in one basket. They wouldn't fit. Nikky, 9, of Hinsdale, Illinois, sells as many as seven dozen eggs a day. When she began keeping chickens as pets four years ago, she gave the eggs away. Now Nikky has about 25 customers who buy them on a regular basis. "People like my eggs because they are so good and so fresh," she says. Nikky spends several hours a day caring for chicks and feeding, cleaning, and playing with her hens. For Nikky it's a labor of love. "My chickens are my friends," she explains.

Looking It Up

You can find answers to some questions in the dictionary. A dictionary is a book about words. The words are arranged in alphabetical, or ABC, order.

A dictionary can show you how to spell a word. It can also tell you what a word means. Sometimes a word has more than one meaning.

E
e

energy
Energy is what makes things happen. Heat, light, and electricity are forms of **energy**. —**energies**

engine
An **engine** is a kind of machine. It burns oil, gas, or wood to do work. Cars, ships, and planes have **engines** to make them move.

engineer

engineer
1. An **engineer** is a person who drives a train. **Engineers** work the engines in the front of trains.
2. An **engineer** is also someone who tells people how to make engines, machines, or buildings.

enjoy
To **enjoy** something means to like it. We all **enjoyed** our vacation this year. We especially **enjoy** vacations in the country.

enough
Enough means as much or as many as you need. We have **enough** food for everybody.

Guide words tell you the first and last word defined on the page.

The **definition** of the word explains what the word means.

This word has **two meanings.** You can decide which meaning best fits how a word is used.

81

Be a Mapmaker!

You know how to read and use maps. Now follow these steps to make a map of a real place.

1 Decide what your map will be about. These children are mapping some of the stores in their community.

2 Find out where everything is. A simple drawing of the place will help you remember where things are.

3 Find out which way is north. Mark it on your drawing. Write it in your notes.

4 Use your notes and drawings to make your map. Decide which symbols you will use in your map key. Be sure to include a compass rose!

Store

Post Office

Bank

Supermarket

News Stand

Movie Theater

Ice Cream Parlor

Book Store

Parking Lot

83

Piggy Bank $ave

Saving money is a good habit.
One place to begin saving
is a piggy bank. Here are the steps
to follow to make your own piggy bank.

You need:

pipe cleaners

markers

milk jug

corks

glue

Glue

scissors

felt

Save your money and fill up your piggy bank!

1 Start with a clean empty milk jug. Put the jug on its side. Cut a big enough slit on the top of the jug to fit coins.

2 Cut four circles for feet.

3 Push the corks in firmly. Add glue if you need to.

4 Use felt, a pipe cleaner, crayons, and markers to decorate your pig.

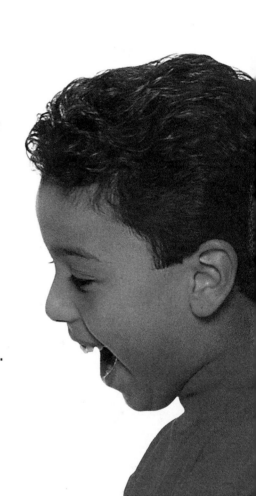

85

Money Over Time

Could you buy a pair of  or a

sneakers   sandwich

with  ? Long ago that is just what

beads

people did. People used these objects for money.

large stone   metal key   cowrie shells

Here is how money looks  today.

86

We Learn

Our Rules And Laws

We Learn Our Rules and Laws

Table of Contents

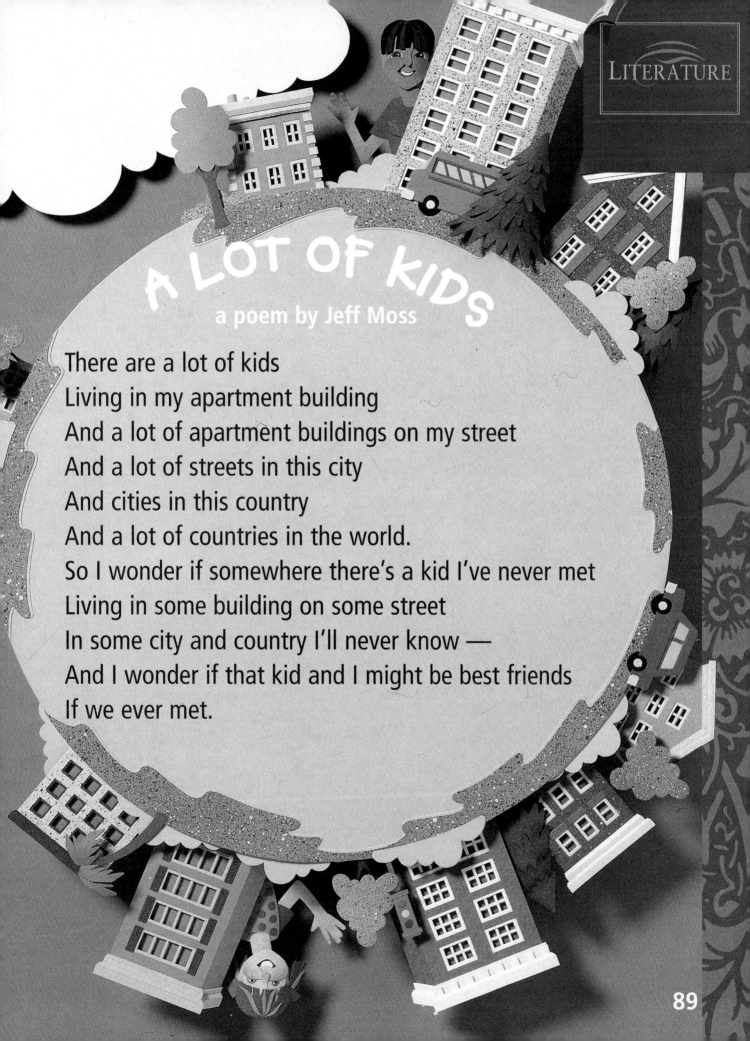

A LOT OF KIDS

a poem by Jeff Moss

There are a lot of kids
Living in my apartment building
And a lot of apartment buildings on my street
And a lot of streets in this city
And cities in this country
And a lot of countries in the world.
So I wonder if somewhere there's a kid I've never met
Living in some building on some street
In some city and country I'll never know —
And I wonder if that kid and I might be best friends
If we ever met.

Culture Fair

The United States of America is made up of people from all different cultures. These children are sharing music, stories, and ideas.

What you believe in, the languages you speak, what you do, and the group of people you belong to make you part of a culture. Can you tell what cultures these children are celebrating?

Culture Quilt

Make a culture quilt with your class. Each student will make one oak tag square. Then you will put all your squares together.

Here's What You Need
tissue paper
construction paper
ribbon
macaroni
cotton balls
foil
pieces of cloth
scissors
glue

Here's How

- **Use your materials to make symbols that tell about your own culture or a culture you know about.**

- **Arrange your symbols on the oak tag square.**

- **Glue the symbols onto the square. Write your initials in the corner.**

- **Tape all the squares together to make a culture quilt.**

How Many Cultures?

Can you guess how many cultures there are in your class?

Here's How

- **Ask your family where their families lived before coming to the United States.**

- **If your family is Native American, ask the name of the group they belong to and where they live.**

- **Write each place name on a self-stick note. Write your initials on the note.**

- **Stick all your notes onto a world map.**

- **How many countries and groups do you see? Share your own culture.**

What Do

People from all over the world have come to live in the United States. Long ago, many people left their homes in other countries and sailed to New York City on large ships. What did they see when they came to the city so long ago?

You See?

Look at the picture on the left. It shows New York City as it looked many years ago. The photograph above shows the city as it looks today. What is the same? What is different? Look at the details in each picture.

Coming Together

Native Americans were the first people to live in North America. People come to the United States from many parts of the world. People move to all states. Many people move to California, New York, Texas, Florida, and New Jersey. These states are colored purple on the map.

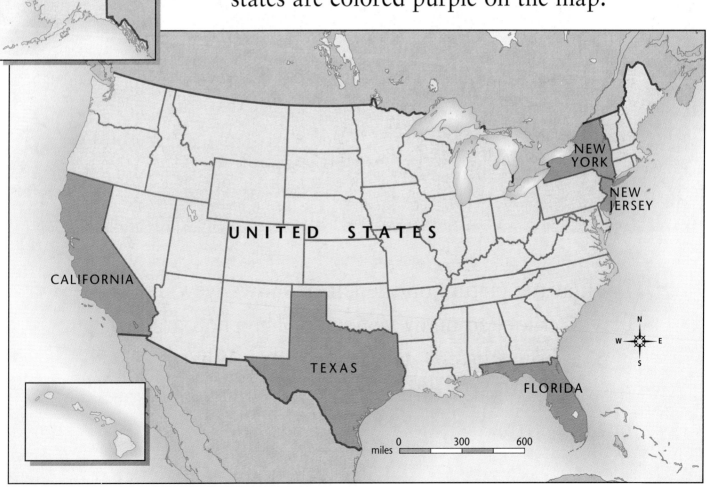

CALIFORNIA

UNITED STATES

NEW YORK

NEW JERSEY

TEXAS

FLORIDA

miles 0 300 600

N
W E
S

All these people come together to live,
to work, and to play. To keep everyone
safe, there are rules and laws.

Who makes the rules and laws for the
people in your community?

RULES!

Every day you follow rules in school. You are probably following more than one rule right now!

Rules tell us what to do and what not to do. They help us get along with one another. The leaders of our school, community, and country make rules to help people live and play together safely. Can you tell what rules are being followed in this community?

Stop signs and traffic lights are helpful to drivers.

Crossing guards make sure crosswalks are safe.

The principal helps make rules in school.

Community signs tell people what to do.

SCHOOL

SCHOOL BUS · SCHOOL BUS
SCHOOL

CURB YOUR DOG

DO NOT PICK THE FLOWERS

Making Fair Rules

What rules can you make to help everyone get along? Read Problems 1 and 2, then choose some solutions to role-play.

Here's How

Problem 1: Your class has one old computer and a brand new color-monitor computer with CD-ROM. Everyone wants to use the new computer.

- **Characters: teacher, two students**

- **Some solutions: On the old computer, student could just do writing assignments. With the CD-ROM computer, students can use the encyclopedia and do their writing assignments.**

Some Solutions
1. make 2 lanes.
2. Pass only on the left.
3. Put up a sign with times.
4. Be polite

Here's How

Problem 2: There are many accidents on the wide, smooth path that circles your town park. People on bikes and roller skates sometimes run into walkers and joggers.

- **Characters:** walker, jogger, bike rider, roller skater

- **Some Solutions:** The walkers and joggers want a rule that says bikers and skaters are not allowed. People on wheels go too fast. The bikers and skaters think this rule isn't fair. They say the people on foot go too slowly and block the path.

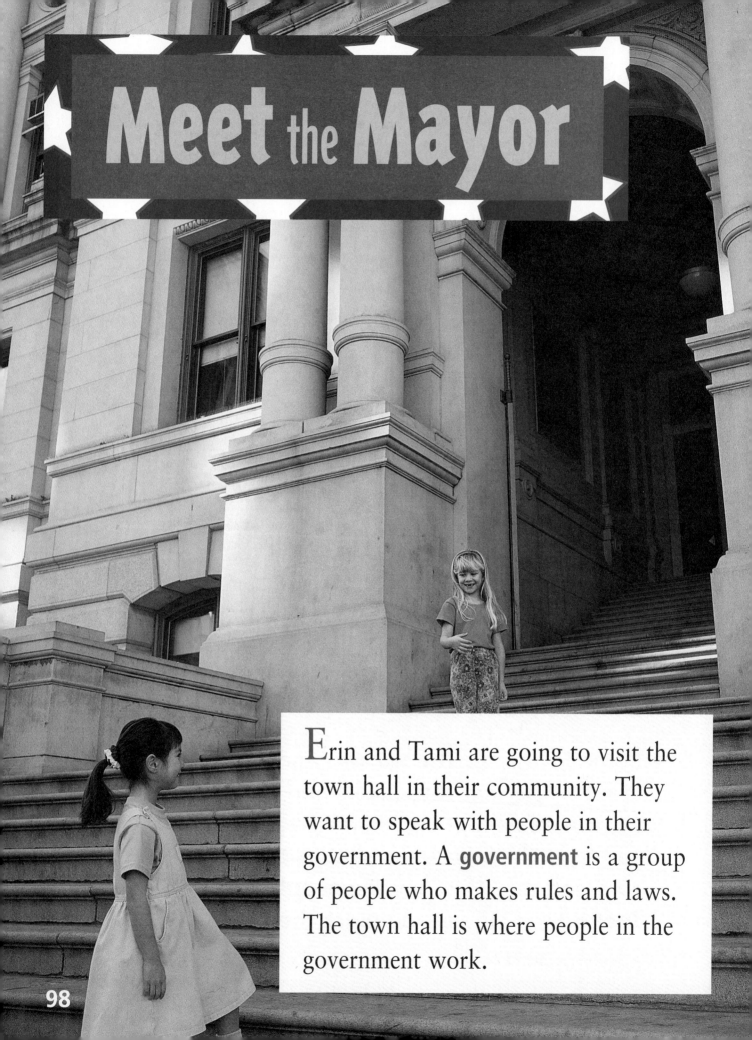

Meet the Mayor

Erin and Tami are going to visit the town hall in their community. They want to speak with people in their government. A **government** is a group of people who makes rules and laws. The town hall is where people in the government work.

In many places the **mayor** is the leader of a town or city government. You can write or visit the mayor if you want to make changes in your community.

Dear Mayor,

I feel there is a problem with the recycling system in our town. We can only recycle number 2 plastic. There are a lot of plastic containers that we have to throw away. Can you tell the recycling company that

The city council is a group of people who helps the mayor solve community problems. They work together to share ideas.

99

Capitol Connection

This is the Capitol Building in Washington, D.C. The Capitol Building is where members of Congress work. **Congress** is a group of people in our government who work together to make laws for the country. A **law** is a rule that people agree to obey. Americans vote for, or choose people to be members of Congress.

The leader of the United States is the **President**. Americans vote every four years to decide who will be President. Sometimes the President comes to the Capitol Building to work with Congress to discuss new laws for our country.

George Washington
First President
1789–1797

Thomas Jefferson
Third President
1801–1809

Abraham Lincoln
Sixteenth President
1861–1865

Theodore Roosevelt
Twenty-sixth President
1901–1909

Dwight David Eisenhower
Thirty-fourth President
1953–1961

John Fitzgerald Kennedy
Thirty-fifth President
1961–1963

Lyndon Baines Johnson
Thirty-sixth President
1963–1969

Who is the President now?

Presidents' Hall

Have you ever been to a living history museum? Here's how to make a Presidents' Hall come alive.

Here's How

- Choose one President. Find a few facts and a picture of that President.

- Draw the President's face on one side of a paper plate. Include as many features of the President's face as you can.

- Write your facts on paper. Tape the paper to the back of the paper plate.

- Hold the paper plate mask in front of your face. Read aloud the sentences you've written.

Getting Around the Capital

Here is a map of Washington, D.C. Look at all the interesting things there are to do in our nation's capital!

Imagine you are going to spend a day there. In small groups, make a travel plan.

Time	Place
10:00 a.m.	Take a tour of the White House. (Try to meet the Preside...
11:30 a.m.	Go to Washington Monume...
12:30 p.m.	Eat lunch on the mall.
1:00 p.m.	See the Vietnam Vetera... Memorial.
3:30 p.m.	Visit the National Air and Space Museum.

Here's How

- With your group, look at the map to decide which places you'd like to visit.

- Decide in what order you will visit each of the places you chose.

- Pick one place to find out more about. Also try to find a picture of it. Tell your classmates what you learned.

Can One Person Make a Difference?

Rosa Parks is one person who helped make her own community, Montgomery, Alabama, a better place to live.

Rosa Parks in 1955.

The Story of Rosa Parks

Many years ago, Montgomery had a law. The law said black people and white people could not sit together on city buses. One day, Rosa Parks was told to go to the back of the bus. Mrs. Parks didn't move. She didn't think the law was fair. She was arrested for breaking the law.

The law was changed in 1956. Rosa Parks could sit anywhere on a city bus.

Many people in Montgomery were angry that Rosa Parks was arrested. They wanted all people to be treated fairly. What would make the city change the law?

Many of the African Americans in Montgomery did not use city buses for a whole year. People also marched to protest the law. Finally, the law was changed. Rosa Parks had made a difference!

Rosa Parks at a Martin Luther King, Jr. Day celebration in San Antonio, Texas.

Can We

We learn that rules and laws in cities and towns help people get along. People who obey rules and laws are cooperating with everyone else. What do you do if there isn't a rule or a law that can help you solve a problem?

These students are discussing which endangered animal their class should help save.

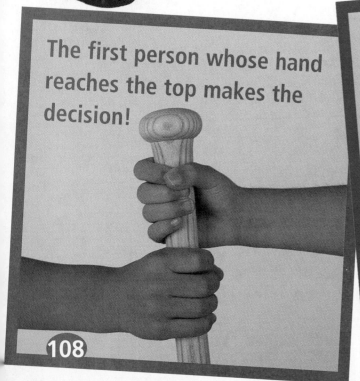

The first person whose hand reaches the top makes the decision!

Try putting names in a hat.

Agree?

One group wants to save the Humpback Whale. Another group wants to save the Green Sea Turtle. The third group wants to save the Red Wolf.

The students want to solve their problem, but they don't know how. Can you think of ways to help them solve this problem?

Save the Sea Turtle

Vote for the Whale

Have you ever flipped a coin?

It's easy to make a ballot and a ballot box!

ballot
☑ red wolf
☐ whale
☐ sea turtle

ballots

What's Your Vote?

One way these students can decide on which animal to save is to vote. **Voting** is one way to choose something. Voting is a fair way to let each person have a say.

ballot

- [ ] red wolf
- [ ] whale
- [ ] sea turtle

Mark your ballot.

There are many different ways to vote. People in The United States vote to make decisions and laws. The President of the United States is **elected**, or chosen by taking a vote.

Voting helps Americans work together to solve problems. They can choose people and laws to help run their communities and the country.

Raise your hand.

Say "yea" or "nay."

Design a Campaign Button

Design a button to show which group you support. Write a slogan to include on your button.

Here's How

- Decide the shape of your button. Outline it on a piece of heavy oak tag. Cut it out.

- Plan your design. Sketch it on a piece of paper. Include your slogan as part of your design.

- Now draw on the oak tag.

- Attach a paper clip to the oak tag. Clip your button onto your pocket, a backpack, or a notebook.

Predict and Tally

What happens when you toss a coin? It comes up heads or tails!

Imagine tossing a coin 50 times. How many times would it come up heads? How many times would it come up tails?

Here's How

- Toss a coin 50 times.

- Each time you toss, record which side lands up.

- How many times did the coin come up heads? How many times was it tails? Was your prediction correct?

The Winning Votes

Everyone has voted to work to save an endangered animal. Which animal got the most votes?

1 First, count the votes. The votes can be grouped by animal.

2 Next, put the information in a table. Tables make information easy to read and understand. Not all tables look like the one shown here. Every table uses rows and columns though.

ballots

112

This is a **table**. It organizes information in rows and columns. The information might be words, numbers, or both.

This is the **title**. It tells what information is on the table.

This is a **column**. Each column has a label, called a **heading**. What are the names of the column headings?

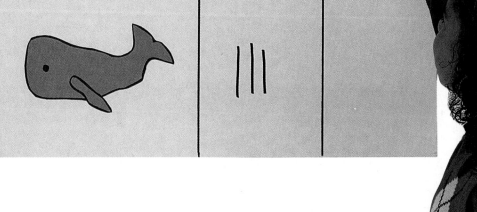

How We Voted

Animal	Tally	Total
🐢	ⅢⅢⅠ	6
🐺	ⅢⅢⅡⅡ	7
🐋	ⅢⅠⅠ	

This is a **row**. What information is in this row?

Can you imagine a time when not many people worried about rain forests or recycling? It was not so long ago.

People realized that the earth needed help. A special day was planned just for the earth.

The first Earth Day was on April 22, 1970. Over 20 million people in the United States celebrated the first Earth Day.

Day

Today, Earth Day is celebrated by more than 200 million people all over the world! Now, many people pay attention to the earth — every day.

People are always finding new ways to help the earth. Some people work to save endangered animals. Other people plant trees.

People worked hard to plan that first Earth Day so many years ago. Now we have a reminder every April 22 — to work together for the planet we share.

Earth Poems

Write a poem
about the earth.

"The Earth"
Birds
Bees
Flowers
Trees
Be Kind to the Earth
If you please.

"My sky"
The sky is high.
I'd like to fly.
Like a bird
way up high.

"I like to climb a tree"
When the sun comes out
I like to shout.
I like to climb a tree
to see what I can see.

Here's How

- **Work with a partner to brainstorm some earth words. Here are some:**
  sun   grass   trees   moon
  whales   ocean   owls   seeds

- **Use one or more of your earth words. Or, use these sentences to begin your poem.**
  The sun is as warm as _____.
  The grass is as green as _____.
  The whale is as big as _____.
  The ocean is as deep as _____.

- **Give your poem a title. Then share it with a friend.**

Earth Day Art

Get together with a friend. Work together to make an Earth Day poster.

Here's What You Need
dried beans
pebbles
shells
twigs
sand
feathers
leaves

Here's How

- Sketch your design onto a piece of cardboard.
- Decide how you will use the items above on your poster. Experiment by putting things in different places.
- Glue your earth things in place. Add color with markers or crayons.

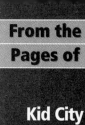

Children of

Aloha! The sun is shining, the sea is blue and the surf's up. Welcome to Hawaii where nature is bold, beautiful and everywhere.

Meet the kids of Heeia Elementary School. They are an example of what Hawaiians call "Na Keiki 'O'Kaina" (say nah kay-EEK-ee oh-kah-EE-nah). It means "Children of the Land."

With the help of Mr. Tagawa, kids at Heeia learn many important lessons about nature. They live up to their name by adopting parks and beaches to clean and beautify.

Read on and see the difference these kids are making in their environment.

the Land

Plant Power

Mr. Tagawa (his students call him Mr. "T") explains how to grow native Hawaiian plants.

Young *naupaka* (say now-PAH-ka) and coconut plants are kept in small pots. Then the plants are taken down to the beach for transplanting.

Native Hawaiian plants slow down the wearing away of the beach by the sea and the wind. This is a young naupaka plant.

Get The Job Done!

On clean-up day, Mr. "T" makes sure everybody gets the job done right. First, the kids clear an area of land. Then they dig holes for the rich soil and plants. The plants are put in the ground and watered.

Mr. "T" points to plants to take to the beach.

In The Heap

The kids keep a compost heap at school. They dump plant and vegetable waste into large wooden boxes. After sitting in the sun and rain for awhile, the compost breaks down and turns into rich soil.

Soil from the compost heap is fertilizer for the plants.

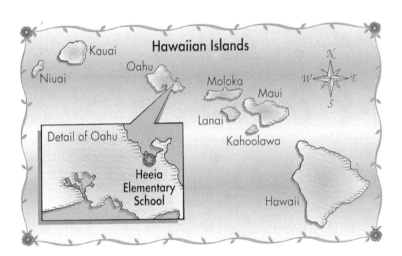

Hawaiian Islands

Kauai

Niuai

Oahu

Moloka

Maui

Lanai

Kahoolawa

Detail of Oahu

Heeia Elementary School

Hawaii

Collectors

After planting, the class walks the beach looking for trash. They sort and collect what people thoughtlessly leave behind. Often they find things like shells, shark's teeth and sea creatures.

Cleaning the beach is an important Earth lesson.

119

Make a Product Map

This map shows farm products produced on the island of Oahu.

Make a product map for one of the other islands.

Here's How

- Decide which island you want to show. Draw an outline of that island.

- Cut it out and paste it on blue paper.

- Label your island. Decide what symbols you will use for its different products.

- Draw the symbols on your map. Make a map key to show what each symbol stands for.

A Hawaiian Lei

If you were to visit Hawaii, you might be given a lei, or a wreath of flowers or shells, that is worn around the neck. You can make your own lei.

Here's What You Need
string or heavy thread
blunt needle
colored tissue paper
straw or tube pasta

Here's How

- Use tisssue paper to make several flowers.

- Thread the needle, then alternate stringing flowers, straws, or pasta.

- Tie the ends of the string together. Place the lei around your neck. Or, give the lei to a friend or family member.

- Don't forget to say "Aloha!"

Part of the Family

a song by Lois LaFond

You don't live next door.
You don't stay at my house.
You don't share my desk
or my bike or my room
You may not even know my name.

But you're part of the Family
Part of Humanity.
We are Brothers & Sisters
All around the globe
All around the globe.

Who is my neighbor?
I am your neighbor.
Who is my sister?
I am your sister.
Who is my brother?
I am your brother.
Who is my neighbor?

Who is my neighbor?
Qui est mon voisin?
C'est moi! (French)
Kto mou coceg?
Ya! (Russian)
¿Quién es mi vecino?
¡Soy yo! (Spanish)
Da-re-ga to-mo-da-chi?
Wa-ta-shee
Bo-koo (Japanese)

Welcome to CANADA

UNITED STATES

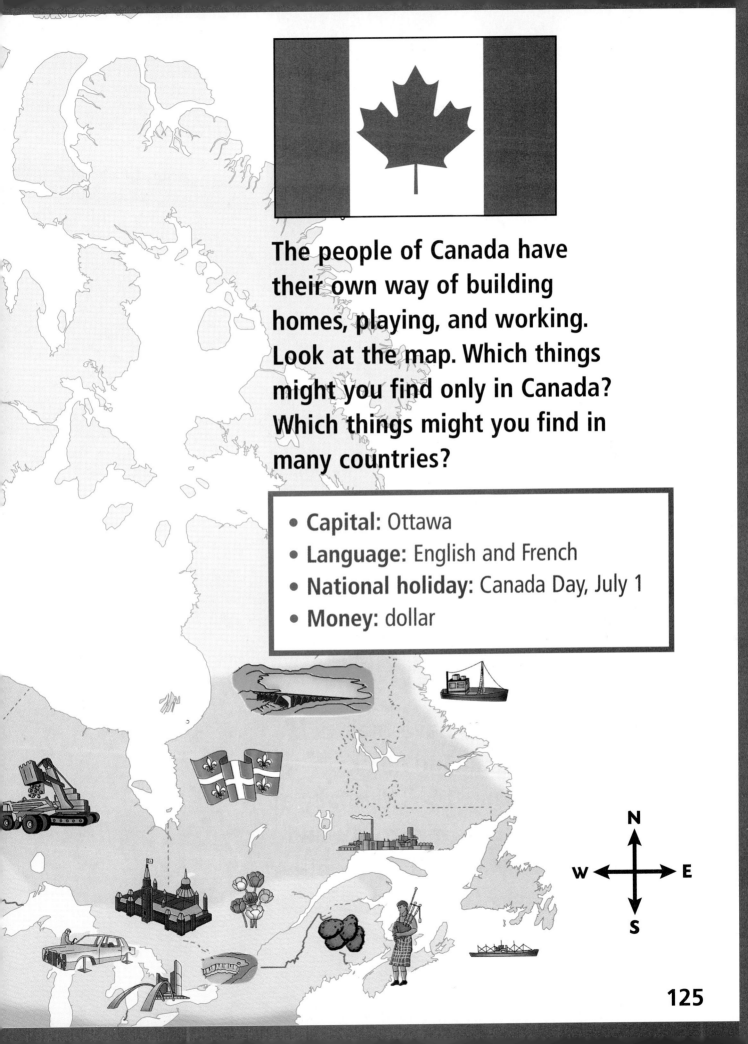

The people of Canada have their own way of building homes, playing, and working. Look at the map. Which things might you find only in Canada? Which things might you find in many countries?

- **Capital:** Ottawa
- **Language:** English and French
- **National holiday:** Canada Day, July 1
- **Money:** dollar

Welcome to
MEXICO

The people of Mexico have their own way of speaking, building homes, playing, and working. Look carefully at the map. Which things might you find only in Mexico? Which things might be the same in Mexico and in other countries?

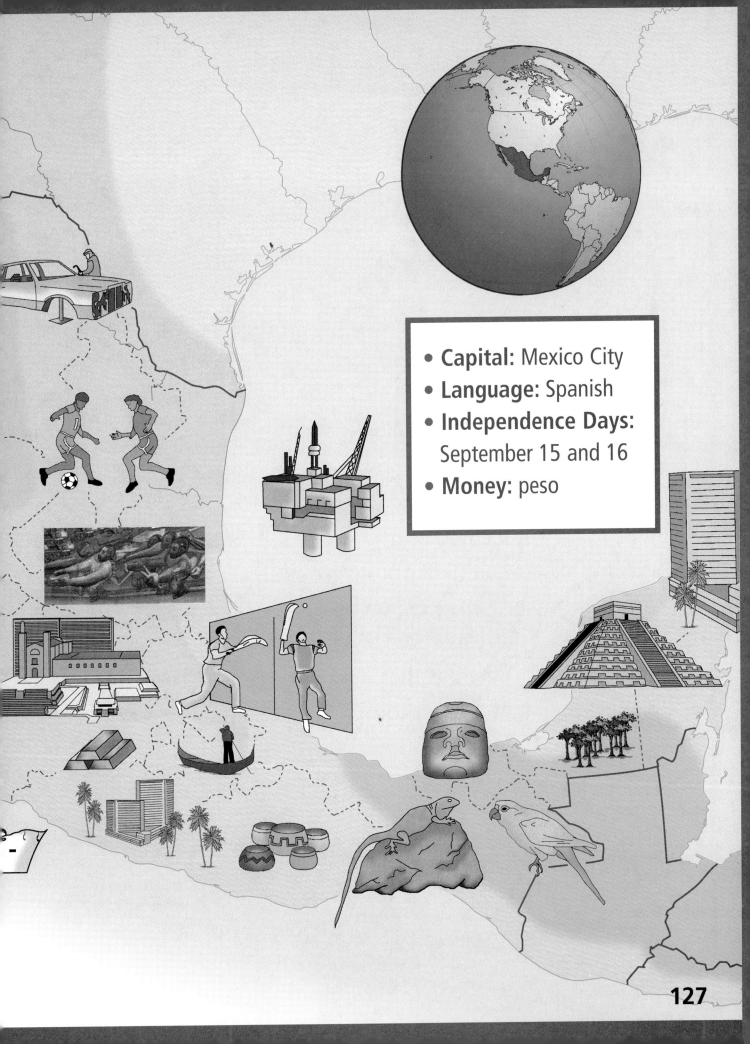

- **Capital:** Mexico City
- **Language:** Spanish
- **Independence Days:** September 15 and 16
- **Money:** peso

Make a Region

A **region** is a place that people create and name. There are many types of regions. They can be different sizes and shapes. When you put a chalk or a string circle around you on the ground, you make a very small region of your own. Your classroom is a second grade region. Where is the playing region at your school?

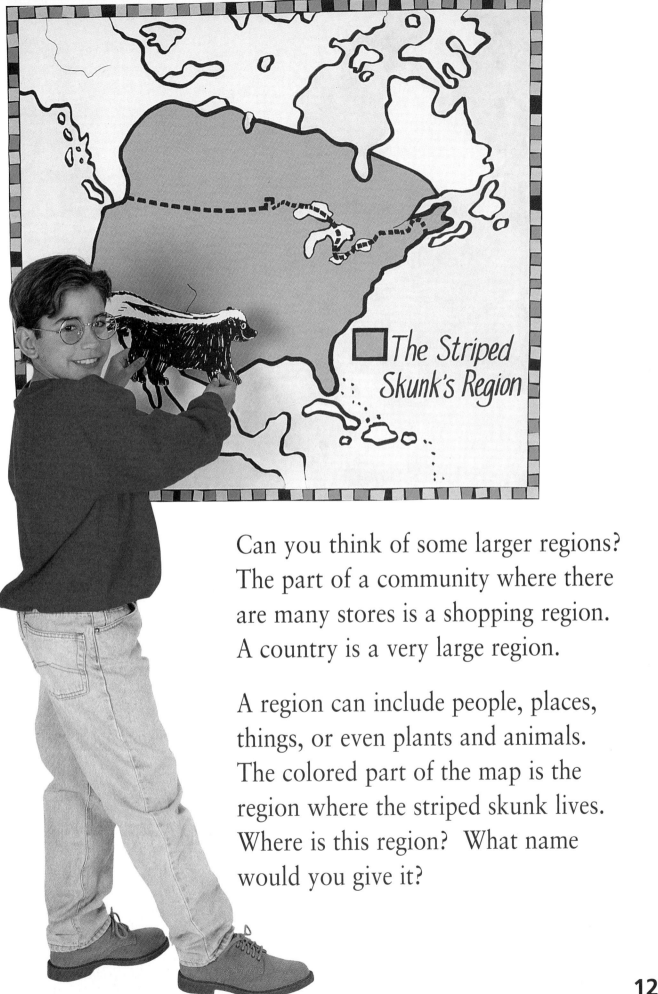

The Striped Skunk's Region

Can you think of some larger regions? The part of a community where there are many stores is a shopping region. A country is a very large region.

A region can include people, places, things, or even plants and animals. The colored part of the map is the region where the striped skunk lives. Where is this region? What name would you give it?

129

50 SIMPLE THINGS KIDS CAN DO TO SAVE THE EARTH

The EarthWorks Group

EARTH FUN FACTS

The average American uses seven trees a year in paper, wood, and other products used from trees. That's over one and a half billion trees a year!

If every person in the U.S. planted a couple of seeds, there would soon be more than 250 million more plants growing and making the Earth a healthier place to live.

If everyone in the U.S. recycled their Sunday newspapers (including the comics), we'd save 500,000 trees every week.

Every year American cars drive a trillion miles. How many is that? Well, it would take you your whole life just to *count* that high!

We Explore

Community Changes

We Explore Community Changes

Table of Contents

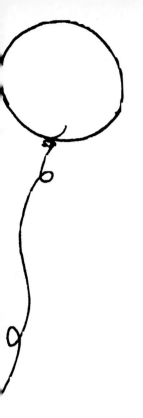

ATIONS
a poem by Shel Silverstein

If we meet and I say, "Hi,"
That's a salutation.
If you ask me how I feel,
That's consideration.
If we stop and talk awhile,
That's a conversation.
If we understand each other,
That's communication.
If we argue, scream and fight,
That's an altercation.
If later we apologize,
That's reconciliation.
If we help each other home,
That's cooperation.
And all these ations added up
Make civilization.

(And if I say this is a wonderful poem,
Is that exaggeration?)

Here We

Everyday you grow and change. As time passes by, you begin to do new things. You learn new ways of communicating, or sending someone a message. You also learn new ways of getting from one place to another.

"Waa Waa"

"Ma Ma"

"I want a cookie."

"Look at me!"

Grow

Look at the bottom of the page. Here are some ways you communicate and move around from the time you are born until you are a teenager.

"It's my first day of school!"

"Where's my bicycle helmet?"

"Watch this turn!"

"May I borrow the car tonight?"

Time on a Line

Do you remember when you first learned to crawl or walk? A **timeline** can help you remember. A timeline is a type of picture that tells what happened and when it happened.

This timeline is a straight line divided into equal parts. Each part marks a year. Events that happen in your first five years are marked on the time line.

What happens in the first year? What things happen over five years?

0   1   2   3   4   5

Eight Months
crawling

One Year
walking

Four Years
skipping

Five Years
bicycle riding

Travel Through Time

This timeline shows how transportation in the United States has changed over time. The timeline goes from the year 1760 to the year 2000. What types of transportation are still used today?

1780 A coach pulled by horses was one way to travel the bumpy dirt roads in the new United States.

| 1760 | 1770 | 1780 | 1790 | 1800 |

1770 Some Native Americans taught explorers how to make birch-bark canoes.

1830 The *Best Friend* was one of the first train engines made in the United States.

1840 Settlers traveled west across the country in covered wagons pulled by horses or oxen.

| 1810 | 1820 | 1830 | 1840 | 1850 |

1814 Many steamboats on the Mississippi and Ohio rivers carried passengers and cotton.

1850 A fast clipper ship could sail across the Atlantic Ocean in about 12 days.

1903 Wilbur and Orville Wright built and flew the first plane in the United States.

| 1860 | 1870 | 1880 | 1890 | 1900 |

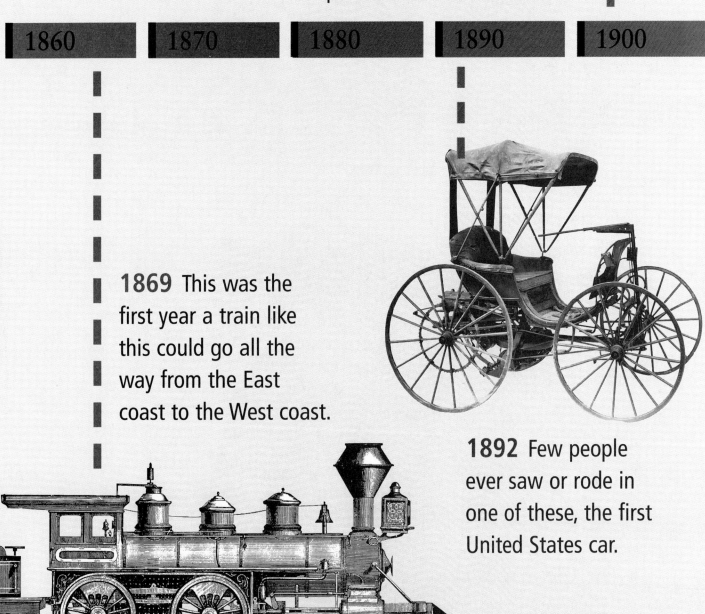

1869 This was the first year a train like this could go all the way from the East coast to the West coast.

1892 Few people ever saw or rode in one of these, the first United States car.

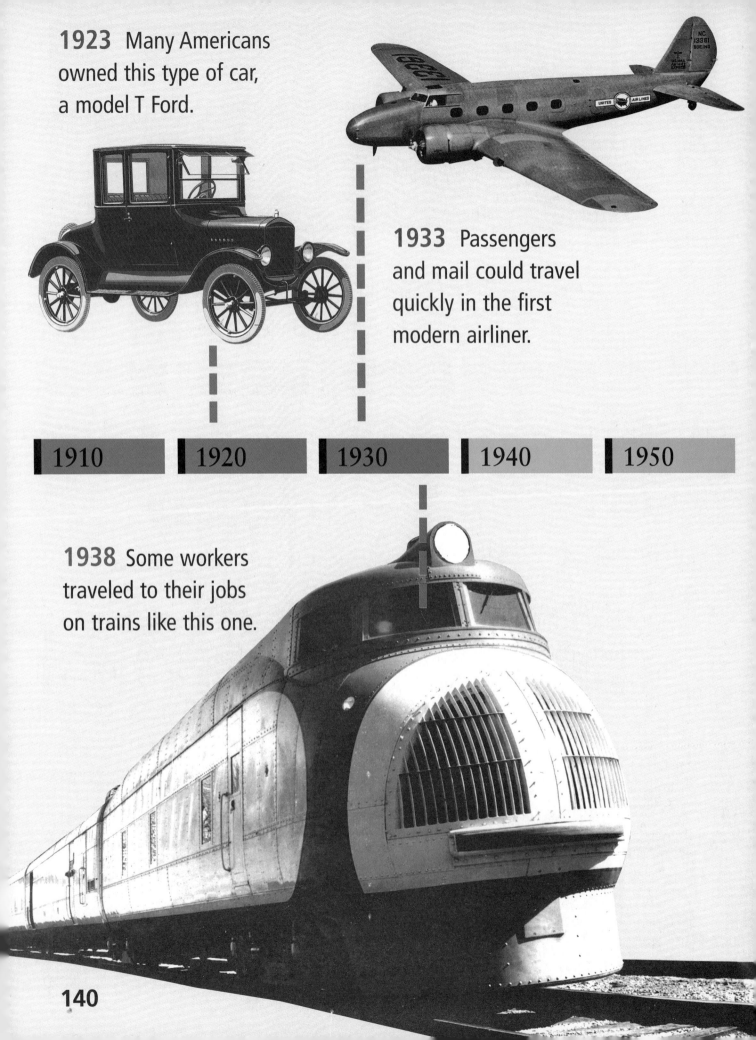

1923 Many Americans owned this type of car, a model T Ford.

1933 Passengers and mail could travel quickly in the first modern airliner.

| 1910 | 1920 | 1930 | 1940 | 1950 |

1938 Some workers traveled to their jobs on trains like this one.

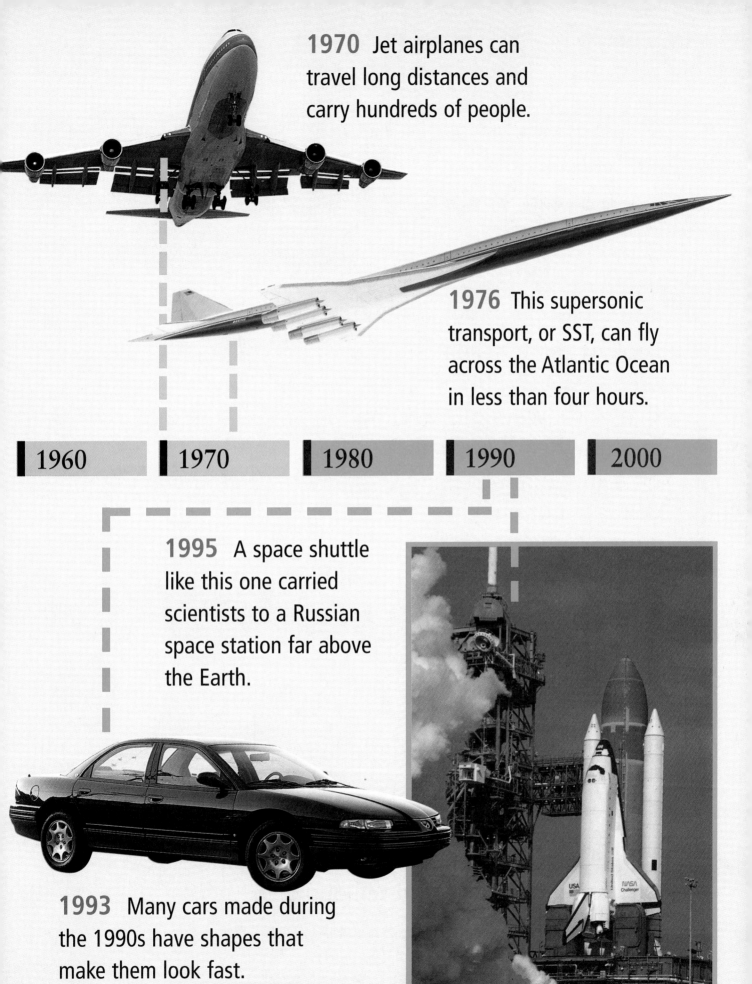

1970 Jet airplanes can travel long distances and carry hundreds of people.

1976 This supersonic transport, or SST, can fly across the Atlantic Ocean in less than four hours.

1960	1970	1980	1990	2000

1995 A space shuttle like this one carried scientists to a Russian space station far above the Earth.

1993 Many cars made during the 1990s have shapes that make them look fast.

A Travel Mobile

Here's How

- Look at the timeline on pages 137–141. Choose five or six ways of traveling and draw each of them on a sheet of oak tag. Cut out your drawings.

- Tie a piece of yarn through a hole in each cut-out drawing.

- Tie the other end of the yarn around a wire hanger or a cardboard tube. Hang your cutouts at different lengths.

- Display your mobile and tell about it.

What Makes It Fly?

How do airplanes stay up in the air? Here's an experiment you can do to find the answer.

Here's How

- Cut a strip of paper two inches wide and eight inches long.

- Hold the end of the paper in one hand. Think: If you blow air over the top of the paper, will the paper move up or down? Make a prediction.

- Now hold the strip of paper in front of your lips. Blow softly. Then blow with a lot of force. Which way did the paper move? Was your prediction correct?

The Powhatan Bus

Henry Bond burns the wooden log.

Meet Henry Bond. His great grandmother was a Cherokee. Henry Bond works at a Powhatan Native American Museum Village. He shows students how the Powhatan people lived.

Wooden chisel and oyster shells

Here's what Henry had to say about transportation:

" Right now, I'm working on a dugout canoe. I'm using the same tools a Powhatan would use: fire, seashells, and a wooden chisel. "

" My favorite part of my job is working with the kids. I ask them how they got here and they say, 'the bus.' I ask them if they want to see the Powhatan bus, and they get all excited. Then I show them the canoe. I tell them that was also the plane, car, train ... everything. "

" Kids are usually surprised that the Powhatans didn't have horses. Horses weren't here yet. For transportation, the Powhatans had canoes like the ones I'm making — and their two feet. "

After the log is burned, it is easy to carve into a canoe.

Getting Here and There

Here is Colonel Pierre Boy outside his school in 1920.

Wagons like this one were used around 1920.

Katie is in second grade and lives in Connecticut. Katie's grandfather, who lives in New Hampshire, grew up on a farm in Canada. When Colonel Boy was in second grade, he walked long distances to school. His family had a horse and wagon to travel to town.

Here is Katie with her grandparents, mother, brothers, and dog, Pipper.

Katie travels in all these ways — car, bus, train, boat, and airplane. "I like to ride my bicycle and skate with my friends," says Katie.

Transportation brings her grandfather closer to her. Katie is happy.

145

Messages from Everywhere

Communication is the way people send and receive messages. Talking and writing are ways to communicate.

When Mrs. Verdugo was in second grade, she wrote letters from her home in Santa Rosalia, Mexico, to family and friends. It took many weeks to receive an answer to her letter. There was only one telephone in her town.

This is Andrés's grandmother, Mrs. Verdugo, in Mexico around 1935.

Today Andrés calls his grandmother from California. Andrés communicates with his cousins in Mexico on his computer. Andrés says, "At home, we speak two languages, English and Spanish." Today it is easy to share ideas quickly with people who live many miles away.

People have been writing letters for thousands of years.

Communication Collage

Make a picture collage to show all the ways in which people communicate.

Here's How

- Draw pictures of people talking, singing, dancing, and communicating in many ways. You can cut out pictures from old magazines if you prefer.

- Arrange your pictures on a piece of oak tag.

- Paste your pictures in place.

- Give your collage a title and display it in the classroom.

Say Hello Around the World

Here's How

- Ask classmates who are from different countries how they say hello in their primary languages.

- Do some research to find other ways to say hello. Make a chart.

- Practice saying hello in different languages.

- Write all the ways you've found to say hello on self-stick notes. Put the notes on a world map, close to where each language is spoken.

Language · How to Say "Hello"

Portuguese - Alô (ah LOH)
French - Allô (ahl LOH)
Japanese - Konnichiwa (Koh nee kee WAH)
Yoruba - Pele (PAY lay)

Place to Place

Would you take an airplane to school? Would you walk from Canada to Mexico? When you travel, you must choose a kind of transportation.

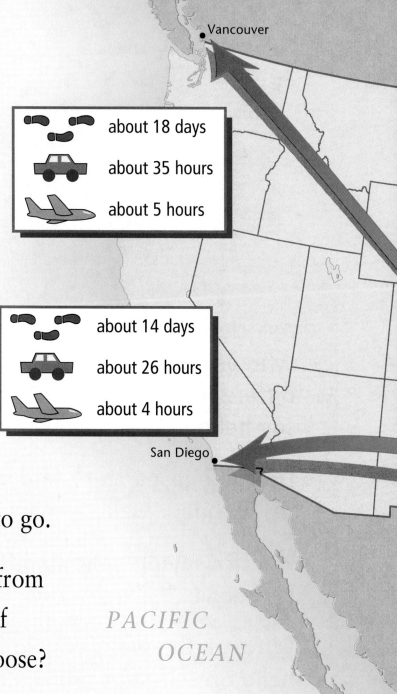

about 18 days

about 35 hours

about 5 hours

about 14 days

about 26 hours

about 4 hours

Vancouver

San Diego

PACIFIC OCEAN

Walking, driving, and flying are forms of transportation. They move you from one place to another. The kind of transportation you choose depends on where you want to go.

Look at these ways to travel from Austin, Texas. Which kind of transportation would you choose?

CANADA

UNITED STATES

about 11 days

about 22 hours

about 2 hours

about 15 days

about 29 hours

about 4 hours

Chicago

Washington, D.C.

ATLANTIC OCEAN

Austin

miles 0   200   400

N
W   E
S

GULF OF MEXICO

Monterrey

MEXICO

about 4 days

about 8 hours

about 1 hour

Looking at Boundaries

A **boundary** is a type of line. When you cross a boundary you go from one place to another. Some boundaries are imaginary. You can see the boundaries of a city, state, or country only on a map. These boundaries show which city, state, or country the land belongs to.

This map shows some boundaries between states and countries. Some of the lines are straight. Others follow the turn of a river, or the curve of a lake. Look for a river boundary between two states, and a river boundary between two countries. What other boundaries can you find?

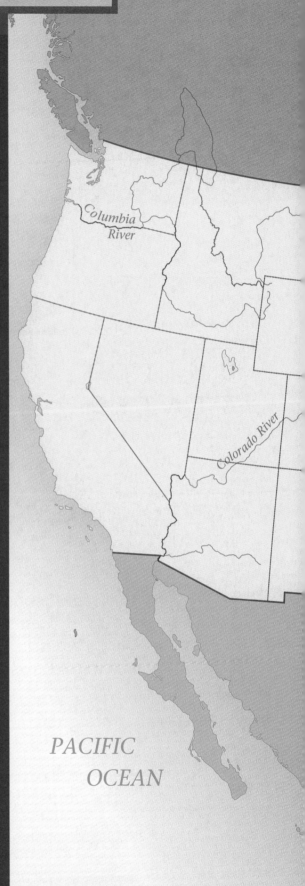

Columbia River

Colorado River

PACIFIC OCEAN

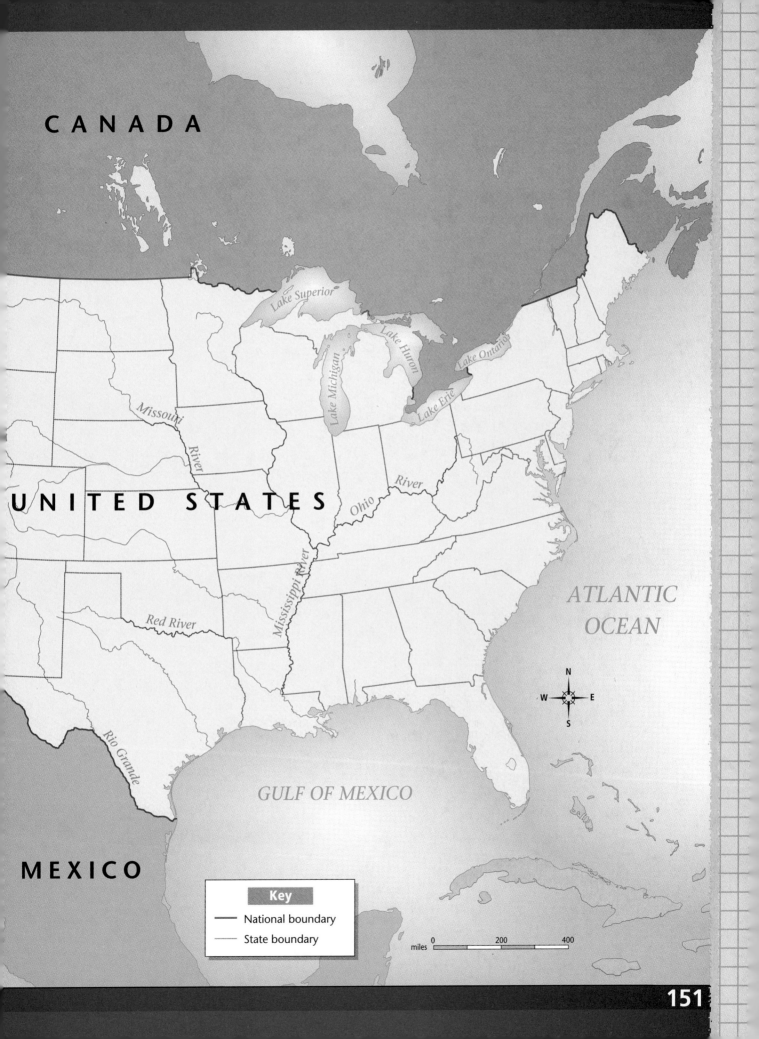

CANADA

Lake Superior

Lake Huron

Lake Michigan

Lake Ontario

Lake Erie

UNITED STATES

Missouri River

Ohio River

Mississippi River

Red River

Rio Grande

ATLANTIC OCEAN

N
W E
S

GULF OF MEXICO

MEXICO

Key

—— National boundary

------ State boundary

miles 0   200   400

Oregon City

5

4
Snake
River

ROCKY

Sweetwater River

3

2

Fort
Laramie

MOUNTAINS

Independence,
Missouri

1

N

W   E

S

152

They Went Thataway!

Long ago, some people in the United States wanted to move west to find new land. Many of these pioneers traveled on the Oregon Trail. They started at Independence, Missouri, and traveled in wagons to Oregon Territory.

Look at the map. See how the trail twists and turns. The travelers crossed rivers, climbed mountains, and searched for drinking water along the way. The trail was the best path the pioneers could take, but the trip was long and hard. What made the trip so difficult?

1. There were no stores on the trail. At Independence, settlers had to buy supplies.

2. It took two months to get to Fort Laramie.

3. At Sweetwater River, the travelers could fill their barrels with drinking water.

4. The pioneers had to cross the Snake River.

5. Oregon City was the first real town the travelers had seen in five months.

Moving the Mail

One way people communicate is by writing letters. Letters help people keep in touch. Here are some of the ways letters were sent to people long ago.

A dogsled delivers the mail.

City mail carriers stop to rest.

A homing pigeon waits for a letter.

Today the United States Postal Service delivers millions of letters. Letters arrive quickly from faraway places. Computers help to sort mail. Jet planes help to transport letters to many communities. Most mail is delivered to our homes by mail carriers who ride in trucks or walk on foot.

A return address prevents letters from getting lost.

Sally Brooks
25 Town Way
Somerville, MA 02145-0998

James Brooks
21 Main Street
Welcome, Massachusetts 12345-1234

A postage stamp pays for mail delivery.

A ZIP code makes sorting mail faster.

Open a Post Office

Set up a post office in your classroom.

Here's How

- **Use boxes to collect mail.**

- **You need these postal workers:**
  Postmaster General:
  In charge of the post office.
  Mail Handlers: Pick up the mail from mail boxes and deliver to the post office.
  Postal Clerks: Sort the mail at the post office.
  Letter Carriers: Deliver letters to each desk.

  Happy letter writing!

Design a Stamp

When the U. S. Postal Service wants to honor a special person or celebrate an event in history, it issues stamps.

What event or person would you like to honor on a stamp?

Here's How

- **Brainstorm with your class a list of people, places, or events you would like to honor.**

- **Choose one idea for a stamp. Draw a sketch.**

- **Draw your stamp on oak tag.**

- **Ask your teacher to photocopy everyone's stamps to display around the classroom.**

"We Could Honor"
- Sam Houston
- Martin Luther King
- John F. Kennedy
- Christa McAuliffe
- George Bush
- Lady Bird Johnson

Symbols

Long ago, some Native Americans told stories by carving pictures and other symbols onto rocks.

Newspaper Rock is a famous petroglyph in Arizona.

The rock carvings are called **petroglyphs.** Today many people use letters of the alphabet to write stories or messages.

Sending a message from one computer to another is called **electronic mail.**

156

Sounds

The sound of bells ringing through a town often signals a message. The Liberty Bell is a famous American landmark. It rang when the United States of America became a free country.

In July of 1776, the Liberty Bell rang at Independence Hall in Philadelphia, Pennsylvania.

What symbols and sounds do you use to send messages?

Talking Hands

People who are hard of hearing or deaf often use sign language to communicate with others. Try these ideas with a partner.

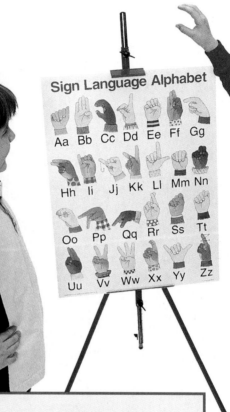

Here's How

- **Use the American Manual Alphabet to fingerspell your name. Next try fingerspelling short sentences, such as "I like you" or "Thank you."**

- **Practice hand signals that might be used to show these things: book, baby, up, car, jump, down, scissors, swim, push.**

157B

Picture This!

Reading a Diagram

A **diagram** is a type of picture that makes it easy to find and name the parts of an object.

A diagram is made up of simple lines. Each object in the diagram is labeled. A straight line connects each part to its label. A title tells what the diagram shows.

The diagram on the right shows some parts of a computer.

What would you like to diagram?

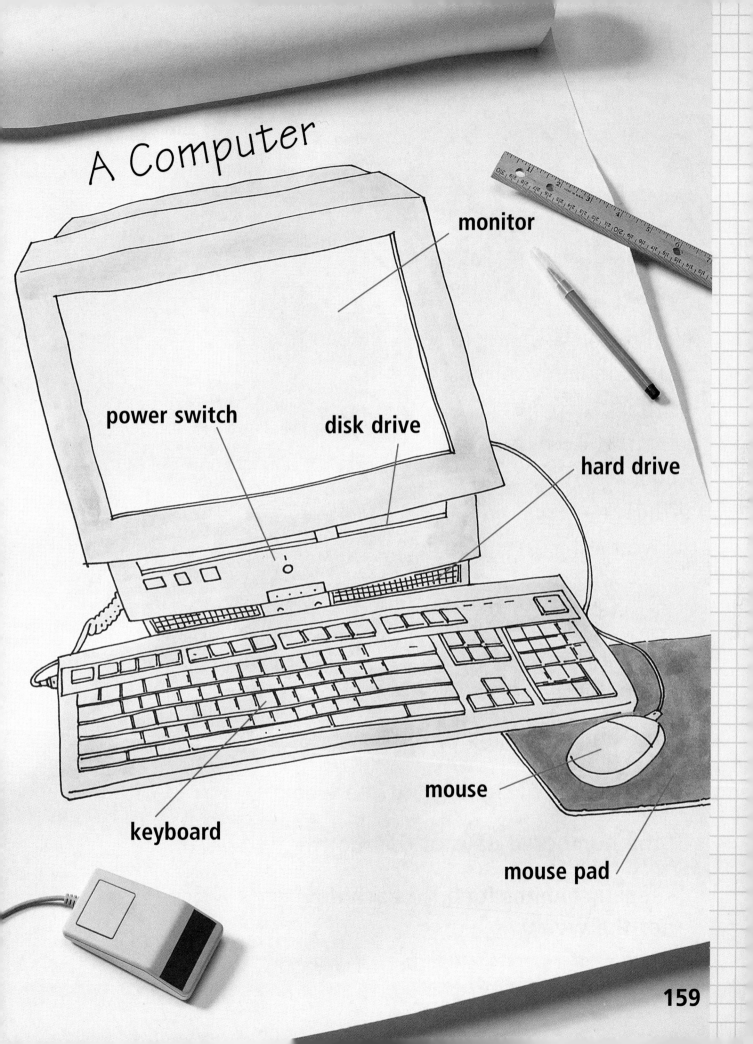

A Computer

monitor

power switch

disk drive

hard drive

keyboard

mouse

mouse pad

A Computer Calendar

Work with classmates to create a monthly calendar on your classroom computer. Keep track of school activities, birthdays — even the weather!

Here's How

Make sure your calendar includes:

- **the name of the month**

- **the names of the days of the week**

- **the numbered days of the month**

- **seven columns (one for each day of the week)**

Two Ways to Tell Time

Figure out the difference between telling time on a digital clock and a mechanical clock.

Here's How

- **The clock on the left is digital.**
  - **The number before the : tells the hour.**
  - **The number after the : tells the minutes.**

- **The clock on the right is mechanical.**
  - **The small (short) hand points to the hour.**
  - **The big (long) hand points to the minutes.**

Which type of clock would you use to teach a younger child to tell time?

What's at B2?

A grid can help you find places and things on a map. A grid is made of straight lines that make squares in columns and rows. Each column has a letter and each row has a number. The letters and numbers name each square. Look at the picture below. The school is in square C2.

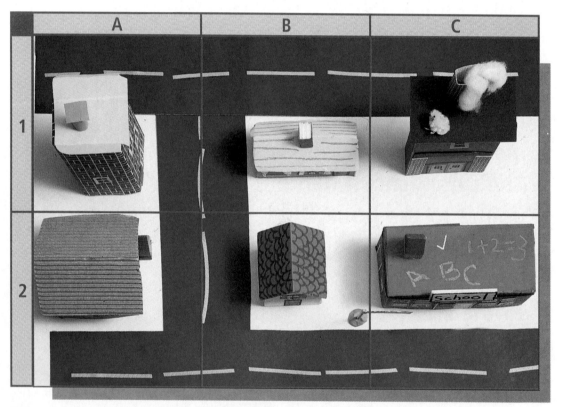

The map on the next page has a grid. A map is a small picture of a larger place. One inch on this map stands for one mile on earth. Mapmakers call that the distance scale. On this map the school and the park are two inches apart. How far apart are they on earth?

160

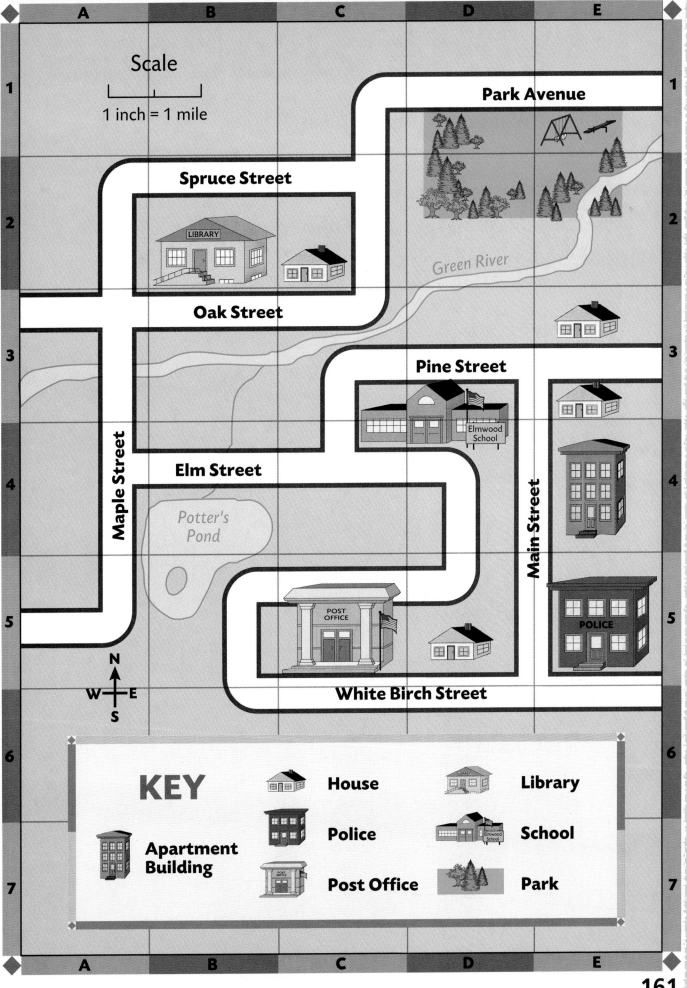

161

Satellite Stations

Have you ever wondered how you can communicate with someone on another continent? One way is through satellites. Satellites can send messages from phones, televisions, radios, and computers.

When people in Dallas, Texas, call Paris, France, telephone wires send messages to a satellite on the ground. The ground satellite beams the messages to a satellite station in space.

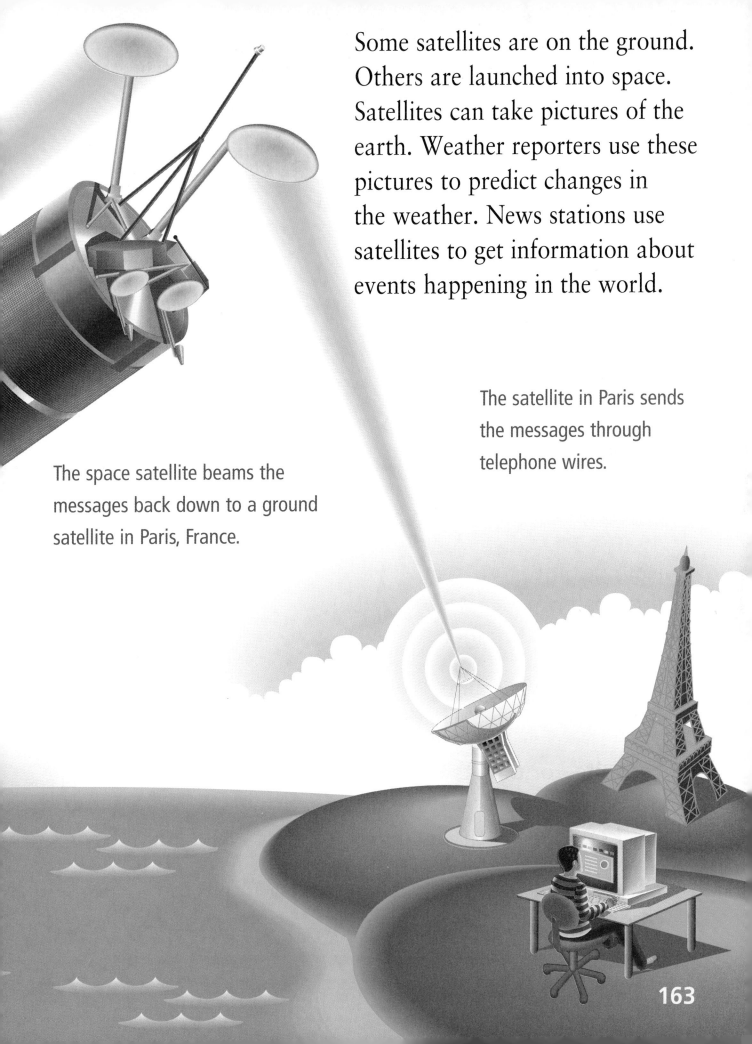

Some satellites are on the ground. Others are launched into space. Satellites can take pictures of the earth. Weather reporters use these pictures to predict changes in the weather. News stations use satellites to get information about events happening in the world.

The satellite in Paris sends the messages through telephone wires.

The space satellite beams the messages back down to a ground satellite in Paris, France.

163

Show a Satellite

With a mirror, flashlight, and large piece of cardboard, you can show how a satellite works.

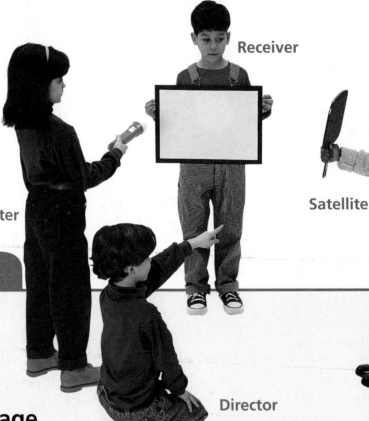

Receiver

Satellite

Transmitter

Director

Here's How

- In groups of four, get into the positions shown on this page.

- The Transmitter aims the flashlight right at the Satellite.

- The Director directs the Satellite to turn until the signal from the Transmitter reaches the Receiver.

- The Director has the Receiver slowly move the cardboard until the signal is right in the center.

Write a Piñata Message

What was your favorite part of the school year? Write a message for next year's second graders — and put it in a class piñata that you make yourself!

I like our teacher. He makes us laugh and learn.

The best p... is learnin... draw ma...

Fridays a... best bec... we sing.

Here's How

- **Write a message on a strip of paper.**

- **Fill a large brown paper bag with crumpled newspaper and all the message strips from your class.**

- **Glue the outside of the piñata with strips of paper you have cut to look like fringe.**

- **Punch holes around the top, thread with yarn, and pull and tie to close.**

Find It in the Library

You can find information in a library.
Look at the different places you might
find information about communication!

A nonfiction book tells about
real people, places, or things.
Nonfiction is grouped on the
shelves by number.

An encyclopedia and a dictionary
are reference books. A computer
encyclopedia also has facts
about many different subjects.

A card catalog or a computer catalog gives the author, title, and subject of all the books in the library.

The librarian helps you find information.

Magazines have fiction and nonfiction stories about people, places, and things.

Books that have made-up stories are called fiction. They are put on the shelves in ABC order by the last name of the author.

Books

a poem by Katherine Edelman

My shelf of books! I love them so!
They take me where I want to go.

Adventure, deeds of every age
Lie captured on the printed page;
Through them I hear the swish of seas,
The wind in lofty mountain trees.
Their magic brings before my gaze
Heroes of stirring, ancient days.
Here in my chair, through day or night,
They lend me wings for daring flight.

I love my shelf of books, they are
Pathways to sun...and moon...and star!

Be a Good Citizen

As you grow, you can do many things to make the world a better place to live. What would you tell future second graders about being a good citizen?

Here's what second graders from Lisbon Central School in Connecticut say:

"Read stories

"Give money for food to the poor."

WE RECYCLE

"**Rake up leaves** for neighbors who are old so they wouldn't have to do it."

"**Plant apple trees** to help the school and Earth."

to children."

"*Help somebody by being a friend to them.*"

"Have people build and be in charge of a very big recycling center."

Tips for Future Citizens
★ Plant flowers.
★ Listen to the rules.
★ Don't do drugs.

169

Time for a Survey

One way you can tell people in the future what your life is like today is to make a time capsule. How do you decide what to put in a time capsule? Take a survey! A survey is a question or set of questions asked of a group of people.

First decide what questions to ask. You might ask your class:

★ **What would you put in a time capsule?**
★ **What would you tell the second graders of the future?**

Next ask your questions and organize the answers. You can make a table or write a paragraph that tells what you find.

170

our voices

cindy's ball

What We Found Out

What kind?	How Many?
newspapers	卌 卌 II
pictures	卌 III
letters	卌 卌
toys	卌 II
money	II
clothes	IIII
seeds	卌 I

Tips for Future Citizens
* Plant flowers.
* Listen to the rules.
* Don't do drugs.

Journal

Create Your Own
Time Capsule!

Time capsules come in all shapes and sizes. Work with a partner or on your own to create a time capsule. Then fill your time capsule with special memories — to be opened by you or someone else sometime in the future.

Try These Ideas!

- **Paint a round or square cereal box.**
- **Decorate and label a shoebox.**
- **Cover a coffee can with colored paper.**
- **Use a clean, empty plastic jug.**

Reference
Databank

Atlas

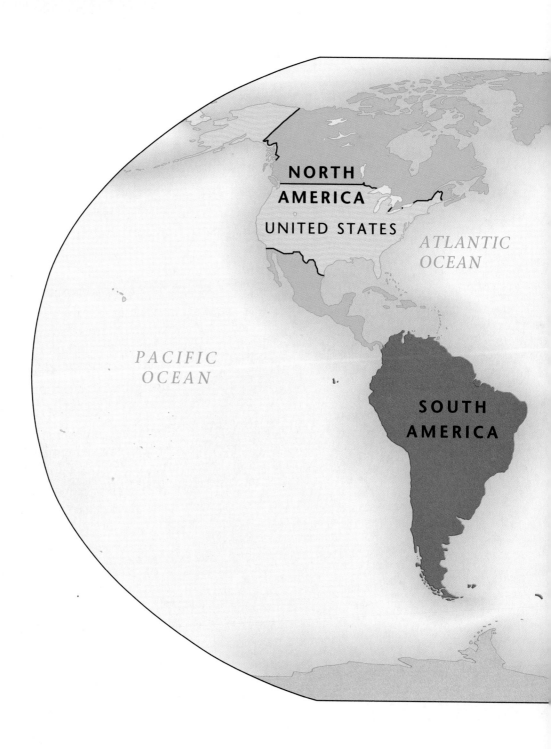

NORTH
AMERICA

UNITED STATES

ATLANTIC
OCEAN

PACIFIC
OCEAN

SOUTH
AMERICA

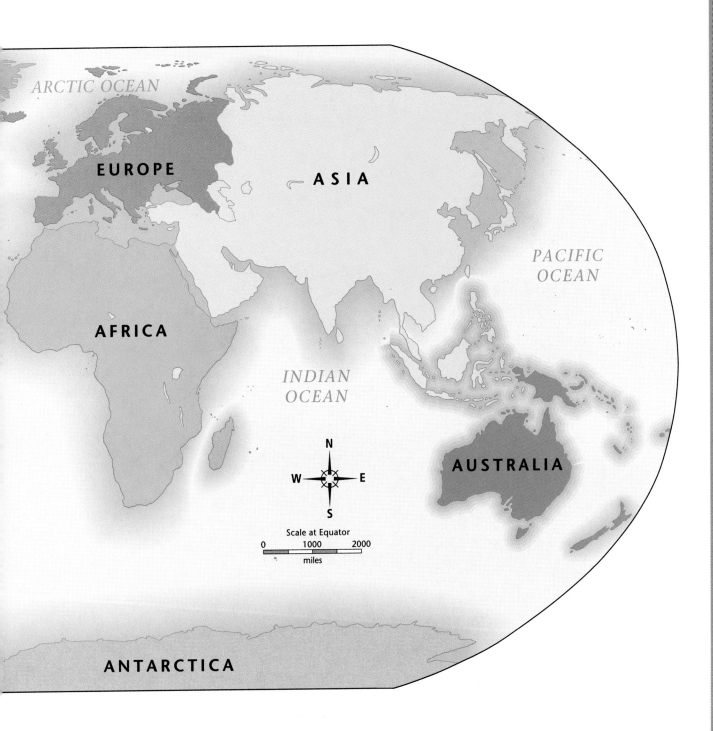

ARCTIC OCEAN

EUROPE

ASIA

AFRICA

PACIFIC
OCEAN

INDIAN
OCEAN

N
W E
S

Scale at Equator
0   1000   2000
miles

AUSTRALIA

ANTARCTICA

175

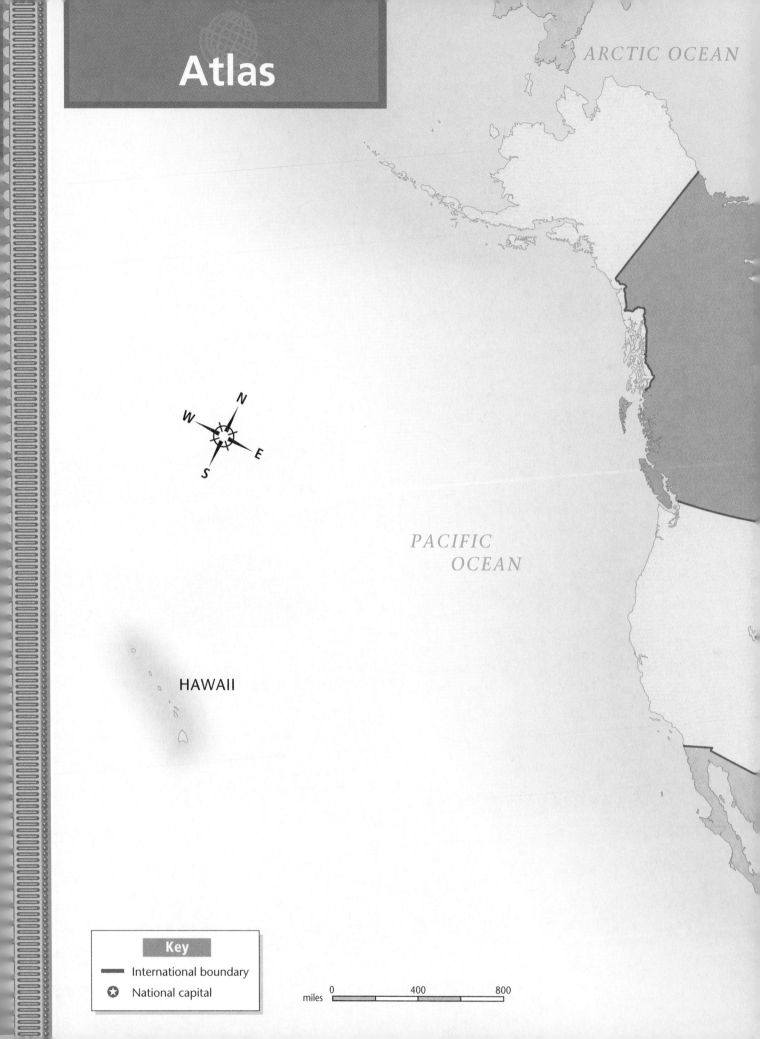

Atlas

ARCTIC OCEAN

N
W E
S

PACIFIC
OCEAN

HAWAII

Key

—— International boundary

⭐ National capital

miles 0   400   800

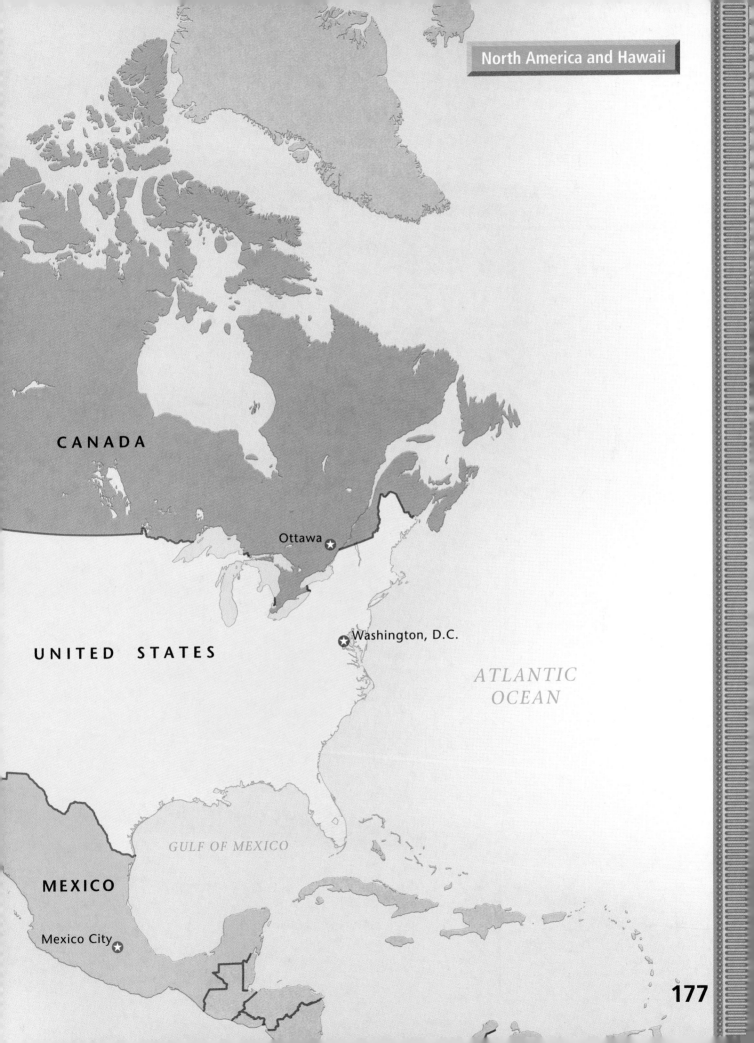

CANADA

Ottawa

UNITED STATES

Washington, D.C.

ATLANTIC
OCEAN

GULF OF MEXICO

MEXICO

Mexico City

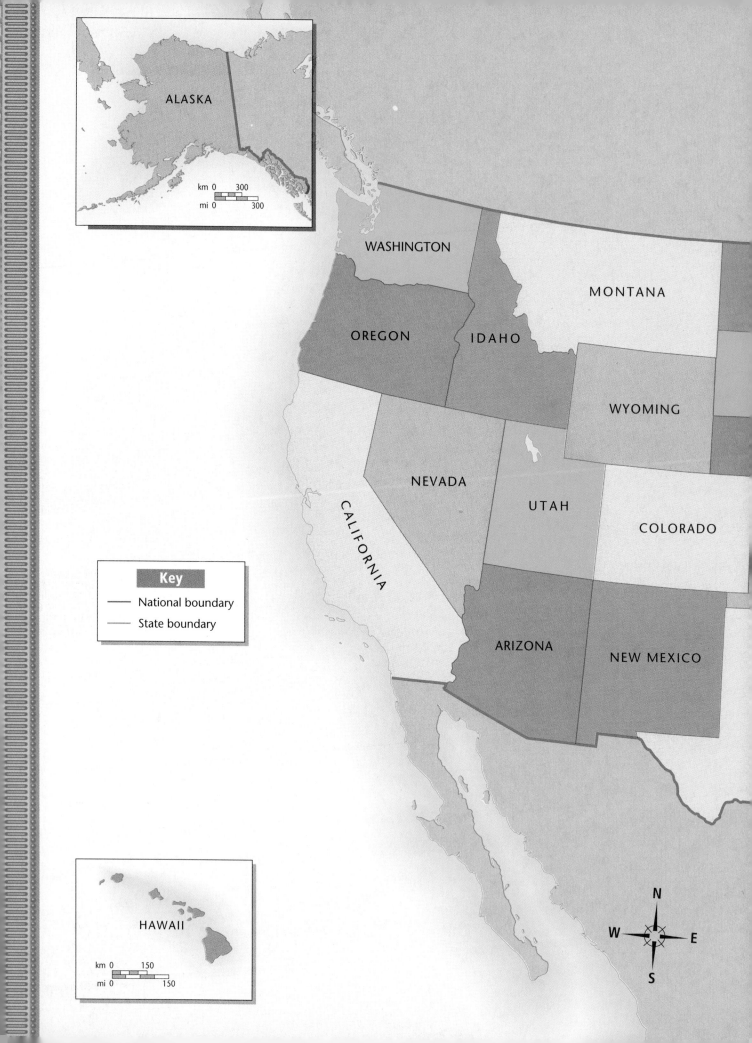

ALASKA

km 0   300
mi 0   300

WASHINGTON

MONTANA

OREGON   IDAHO

WYOMING

NEVADA

CALIFORNIA   UTAH

COLORADO

Key
— National boundary
— State boundary

ARIZONA   NEW MEXICO

HAWAII

km 0   150
mi 0   150

N
W   E
S

NORTH DAKOTA

MINNESOTA

MICHIGAN

MAINE

NEW HAMPSHIRE

VERMONT

SOUTH DAKOTA

WISCONSIN

NEW YORK

MASSACHUSETTS

RHODE ISLAND

CONNECTICUT

IOWA

NEBRASKA

PENNSYLVANIA

NEW JERSEY

ILLINOIS

INDIANA

OHIO

DELAWARE

WEST VIRGINIA

MARYLAND

VIRGINIA

KANSAS

MISSOURI

KENTUCKY

NORTH CAROLINA

TENNESSEE

OKLAHOMA

ARKANSAS

SOUTH CAROLINA

MISSISSIPPI

ALABAMA

GEORGIA

TEXAS

LOUISIANA

FLORIDA

km 0   200   400

mi 0   200   400

© 1996 GEOSYSTEMS GLOBAL CORP.

179

Glossary

Theme 1:
We Build Communities

C

city

A large community where many people live and work. (page 10)

There are tall buildings in a city.

community

A place where a group of people live, work, and follow the same rules and laws. (page 4)

The children picked up trash to keep their community clean.

compass rose

A symbol showing the directions north, south, east, and west. (page 7)

Wendy drew a compass rose on her map.

L

landform

An area of land such as an island or a mountain. (page 28)

The students pointed to the landform on the map.

M

map key

A list of the symbols used on a map. (page 7)

The school is colored red on the map key.

Map Key	
Fire engine	
Store	
Park	
School	

S

suburb

A community near a city. (page 12)

Many of the people who live in the suburb work in the city.

T

town

A community smaller than a city where people live and work. (page 13)

There is a Labor Day parade every year in our town.

trade

To buy, sell, or exchange something. (page 39)

Chen trades baseball cards with his friend Leon.

Glossary

C

consumer

A person who buys things or uses services. (page 57)

*The **consumer** bought some gifts at a crafts fair.*

G

goods

Things that are made or grown and then sold. (page 67)

*Clothes, food, and toys are **goods**.*

I

income

The money people earn for the work they do. (page 71)

*The family's **income** paid for the rent on their apartment.*

N

natural resource

Anything that exists in nature and is useful to human beings. (page 67)

*Water is a **natural resource**.*

needs

Things people must have to live. (page 50)

*Shelter, clothes, food, and love are **needs**.*

P

producer

A person who makes, grows, and sells things. (page 57)

*The **producer** sold what she made at the fair.*

T

taxes

The money people pay to a community or government for services. (page 71)

__Taxes__ help pay for the new road.

V

volunteer

A person who works for no pay. (page 74)

*The **volunteer** is helping out at the hospital.*

W

wants

Things that people would like to have but do not need to live. (page 51)

*Candy and televisions are **wants**.*

Glossary

B

ballot

A piece of paper with a vote written on it. (page 109)

The woman put an X next to her choice on the ballot.

C

Congress

A group of people chosen to make rules and laws for the United States. (page 100)

Congress meets in Washington, D.C.

E

elect

To choose something by voting. (page 111)

The students will elect a class pet.

G

government

A group of people that makes rules and laws. (page 98)

The President is the leader of the United States government.

L

law

A rule that people agree to obey. (page 100)

Our town has many laws.

M

mayor

The leader of a city government. (page 99)

The class wrote a letter to the mayor of their town.

P

President

The leader of the United States and of the American people. (page 101)

The President lives in the White House.

R

region

An area of the earth's surface that people define by a characteristic. (page 128)

Some bears live in the northern region of the United States.

rules

Statements that tell how things or people should behave. (page 96)

To play fair, everyone follows rules.

V

vote

To make a choice as in an election. (page 110)

People vote in elections.

182

Glossary

B

boundary

A real or imaginary line where one place begins and another place ends. (page 150)

*Texas and Mexico share a **boundary.***

C

communication

Any way that people send and receive messages. (page 146)

*Speaking and writing are types of **communication.***

D

diagram

A drawing that shows and names the important parts of something. (page 158)

P204406.02

*Juan made a **diagram** of the classroom.*

E

electronic mail

Messages sent from one computer to another. (page 156)

*The children send **electronic mail** to their pen pals in Puerto Rico.*

P

petroglyph

A carving or line drawing on rock. (page 156)

*Scientists found a **petroglyph** from thousands of years ago.*

T

timeline

A line marked to show the order in which things happen. (page 136)

*Make a **timeline** of all the holidays in a year.*

transportation

Any way of moving people or things from place to place. (page 137)

*Jet planes are fast **transportation.***

Index

Page numbers with *m* before them refer to maps. Page numbers with *p* before them refer to diagrams and graphs and numbers with *c* refer to charts.

Credits

Acknowledgments

For each of the selections listed below, grateful acknowledgment is made for permission to excerpt and/or reprint original or copyrighted material, as follows:

Permissioned Material

Selection from *50 Simple Things Kids Can Do To Save The Earth,* by John Javna. Copyright © 1990 by John Javna. Reprinted by permission of Andrews and McMeel.

"A Lot of Kids," from *The Butterfly Jar,* by Jeff Moss. Copyright © 1989 by Jeff Moss. Reprinted by permission of Bantam Books, a division of the Bantam Doubleday Dell Publishing Group, Inc.

"A Song of Greatness," transcribed by Mary Austin, from *The Children Sing in the Far West.* Copyright © 1928 by Mary Austin. Copyright © renewed 1956 by Kenneth M. Chapman and Mary C. Wheelwright. Reprinted by permission of Houghton Mifflin Company.

p. 91 from *The American Heritage First Dictionary.* Copyright © 1994 by Houghton Mifflin Company. Reprinted by permission. All rights reserved.

Selection from *The American Heritage First Dictionary.* Copyright © 1994 by Houghton Mifflin Company. All rights reserved.

"Ations," from *A Light in the Attic,* by Shel Silverstein. Copyright © 1981 by Shel Silverstein. Reprinted by permission of HarperCollins Publishers.

"Automobile Mechanics," from *I Like Machinery,* by Dorothy Baruch. Every attempt has been made to locate the rightsholder of this work. If the rightsholder should read this, please contact Houghton Mifflin Company, School Permissions, 222 Berkeley Street, Boston, MA 02116-3764.

Book shown with poem "Books," by Katherine Edelman: *The Wooden Man,* by Max Bolliger, illustrated by Fred Bower. Published by Seabury Press/Clarion Books, copyright © 1974 by Artemis Verlag.

"Books," by Katherine Edelman. Copyright © by Katherine Edelman. Reprinted by permission of Katherine Edelman Lyon, Literary Executrix for Katherine Edelman.

"Children of the Land," from *Kid City* magazine, April 1995. Copyright © 1995 by Children's Television Workshop. Reprinted by permission.

Selection from *Colonial Craftsman and the Beginnings of American Industry,* written and illustrated by Edwin Tunis. Copyright © 1965 by Edwin Tunis. Reprinted by permission of HarperCollins Publishers.

"Computer Mouse," from *The Way Things Work,* by David Macaulay. Text copyright © 1988 by David Macaulay and Neil Ardley. Compilation copyright © 1988 by Dorling Kindersley Limited, London. Illustrations copyright © 1988 by David Macaulay. Reprinted by permission of Clarion Books, a division of Houghton Mifflin Company. All rights reserved.

"The Fair in Reynosa," from *Family Pictures,* by Carmen Lomas Garza. Copyright © 1990 by Carmen Lomas Garza. Reprinted by permission of Children's Book Press.

"Fall Arrives," by Martin Shaw, from *Teaching K-8* magazine, August/September 1994. Copyright © 1994 by Teaching K-8, Norwalk, CT 06854. Reprinted by permission.

"Galoshes," from *Stories to Begin On,* by Rhoda Bacmeister. Copyright © 1940, renewed 1968 by Rhoda W. Bacmeister. Reprinted by permission of McIntosh & Otis, Inc.

"Good-Bye, Six- Hello, Seven," from *If I Were in Charge of the World and Other Worries,* by Judith Viorst. Copyright © 1981 by Judith Viorst. Reprinted by permission of Aladdin Books, a division of Simon & Schuster Children's Publishing Division.

"I Don't Want to Live on the Moon," from *The Butterfly Jar,* by Jeff Moss. Copyright © 1989 by Jeff Moss. Reprinted by permission of Bantam Books, a division of the Bantam Doubleday Dell Publishing Group, Inc.

"If I Lived in the Desert," by Barbara Olson, from *Highlights for Children* magazine, September 1989. Copyright © 1989 by Highlights for Children, Inc. Reprinted by permission.

Cover of *Kids Discover:* Solar System, October 1995. Copyright © 1995 by Kids Discover. Reprinted by permission.

"Little Song," from *The Collected Poems of Langston Hughes,* by Langston Hughes. Copyright © 1994 by the Estate of Langston Hughes. Reprinted by permission of Alfred A. Knopf, Inc.

"Maps," by Goldie Capers Smith, from *The Instructor.* Every attempt has been made to locate the rightsholder of this work. If the rightsholder should read this, please contact Houghton Mifflin Company, School Permissions, 222 Berkeley Street, Boston, MA 02116-3764.

"Our History," by Catherine Cate Coblenz, as reprinted in *Child Life* magazine, October 1945. Every attempt has been made to locate the rightsholder of this work. If the rightsholder should read this, please contact Houghton Mifflin Company, School Permissions, 222 Berkeley Street, Boston, MA 02116-3764.

Pages 24-25 of *Cobblestone* magazine, October 1988. Copyright © 1988 by Cobblestone Publishing, 7 School Street, Peterborough, NH 03458. Reprinted by permission.

"Part of the Family," from *One World,* by Lois LaFond. Copyright © 1990 by Lois LaFond and Company, P.O. Box 4712, Boulder, CO 80306, (303)444-7095.

"September," by Edwina Fallis. Every attempt has been made to locate the rightsholder of this work. If the rightsholder should read this, please contact Houghton Mifflin Company, School Permissions, 222 Berkeley Street, Boston, MA 02116-3764.

"September," from *A Child's Calendar,* by John Updike. Copyright © 1965 by John Updike and Nancy Burkert. Reprinted by permission of Alfred A. Knopf, Inc.

"Sweet Job: Kids in Business," from *National Geographic World* magazine, February 1991. Copyright © 1991 by National Geographic World. *World* is the official magazine for Junior Members of the National Geographic Society. Reprinted by permission.

"This is Our Earth," from *This is Our Earth,* by Laura Lee Benson. Copyright © 1994 by Charlesbridge Publishing. Reprinted by permission of Charlesbridge Publishing.

"Trains," from *I Go A-Traveling,* by James S. Tippett. Copyright © 1929 by Harper and Brothers. Reprinted by permission of HarperCollins Publishers.

"The Tree," by Marge Kennedy, illustrated by Ajin, from *Sesame Street* magazine, October 1992. Copyright © 1992 by Children's Television Workshop. Reprinted by permission.

"Who Am I?" from *At the Top of My Voice and Other Poems,* by Felice Holman. Copyright © 1970 by Felice Holman. Reprinted by permission of Simon & Schuster Children's Publishing Division.

Cover of *With Love from Gran,* by Dick Gackenbach. Clarion Books, Houghton Mifflin Company, 1989.

Photo Credits

"American Voices": 2 Lori Adamski Peek/Tony Stone Images 2–3 © 1992 Jeff Gnass/The Stock Market 4–5 © Arthur Tilly 1993/FPG International 5 © Nancy Brown/The Image Bank 6–7 (US flag) Donovan Reese/Tony Stone Images 6–7 (Childrenwith US flags) © Michael Melford 1986/The Image Bank 8 © Michael Melford 1986/The Image Bank **Theme 1:** 15 Kent Knudson/FPG International(ml) 16 Murray Alcosser/The Image Bank(r) Gale Zucker/Stock Boston(bl) 17 Michael Melford/The Image Bank(br) Bruce M. Wellman/Stock Boston(bl) 18 Guiliano Colliva/The Image Bank(b) Joe Bator/The Stock Market(l) Eddie Hironaka/The Image Bank(br) Rich Iwasaki/Tony Stone Images/Chicago, Inc.(tr) 19 Geoffrey Clifford/The Stock Market(ml) Spencer Jones/FPG International(b) 20 Stacy Pick/Stock Boston(tr) Robert Brenner/Photo Edit(mr) Dennis O'Clair/Tony Stone Images/Chicago, Inc.(br) 21 Brian Yarvin/Peter Arnold, Inc.(bl) Harold Sund/The Image Bank(tl) Barrie Rokeach(tm) Arthur D'Arazien/The Image Bank(ml) Ted Horowitz/The Stock Market(m) Frank Rosotto/The Stock Market(br) Alex S. McLean/Landslides(bm) 22 ©Jack Duggins(b) 23 Gordon Chibrowski/C.C. Church Photography(br) ©Karen Mayo(tr) 24 Robert Frerck/Tony Stone Images/Chicago, Inc.(br) 26–27 Vince Streano/Tony Stone Images/Chicago, Inc. 28 Rod Planck/Photo Researchers, Inc.(t) Gary Irving/Tony Stone Images/Chicago, Inc.(b) 29 Larry Ulrich/Tony Stone Images/Chicago, Inc.(t) Alex S. Maclean/Landslides(b) 30 Mark Segal/Tony Stone Images/Chicago, Inc.(b) Tony Stone Images/Chicago, Inc.(t) 31 Wayne Eastep/Tony Stone Images/Chicago, Inc.(b) Jim Wark/Peter Arnold, Inc.(t) 37 William A. Logan/The Image Bank 38–39 Treat Davidson/Photo Researchers, Inc.(m) 38 The Carnegie Library of Pittsburgh(b) 39 The Bettmann Archive(b) 40 The Carnegie Library of Pittsburgh 41 Mark C. Burnett/Stock Boston(b) Heinz Kluetmeier/Time Inc./*Sports Illustrated*(t) 44 George Riley/Stock Boston(tl) Jean-Claude LeJeune/Stock Boston(r) Patti McConville/The Image Bank(bl) **Theme 2:** 48–49 Mark Segal/Tony Stone Images/Chicago, Inc. 54 Photo Edit(bl) 55 John McDermott/Tony Stone Images/Chicago, Inc.(b) 60 Kaz Mori/The Image Bank(l) 60 61 David Wisse/Natural Selection Stock Photography Inc. 60 Walter Hodges/Westlight(r) Alan Kierney/FPG International Lawrence B. Aiuppy/FPG International Brenda Tharp/Photo Researchers, Inc. Dr. Wm. M. Harlow/Photo Researchers, Inc. Lisa Valder/Tony Stone Images/Chicago, Inc. 62 Earl Dibble/FPG International(l) 63 Stuart Dee/The Image Bank(t) 64 Roy Morsch/The Stock Market(t) Courtesy of Louisville Slugger(b) 65 Courtesy of Louisville Slugger(t)(b) Don Mason/The Stock Market(tl) Michael Rosenfeld/Tony Stone Images/Chicago, Inc.(bl) 66 Ken Rogers/Westlight(br) 74–75 Courtesy of Sarah and Robert Mackinnon 76 Paul Gero/©National Geographic Society Martin Harvey/The Wildlife Collection(tl) 77 Jackie Bell/©National Geographic Society 78 ©Paul Gero/National Geographic Society 79 Kevin Horan/©National Geographic Society 86 Bruce Byers/FPG International(b) American Numismatic Society(ml)(m)(mr) **Theme 3:** cover © David Witbeck/Mercury Pictures 92 The Bettmann Archive 93 Jon Ortner/Tony Stone Images/Chicago, Inc. 95 Rafael Macia/Photo Researchers, Inc.(t) 98 ©David Witbeck/Mercury Pictures(l) 99 ©David Witbeck/Mercury Pictures(tr) Nancy Sheehan/Photo Edit(mr) 100–101 Dennis Brock/Black Star 102–103 Lee Corkran/Sygma 104 National Portrait Gallery, Smithsonian Institution/Art Resource, NY(tl) The White House Historical Association(tr) The Granger Collection(br) M.P. Rice/The Bettmann Archive(bl) 105 The Bettmann Archive(tr) ©Roger Atzenweiler/Courtesy of The Truman Library(tl) ©Bachrach Studios(bl) ©Frank Muto/Courtesy of the Lyndon Baines Johnson Library Collection(br) 106 The Granger Collection(br) The Bettmann Archive(tl) 107 UPI Bettmann(tl) Bob Daemmrich/Stock Boston(br) 114 Seymour Chwast(br) ©Paul Davis Studio(bl) U.S. Environmental Protection Agency(bm) 114–115 NASA(m) 115 ©Earth Day USA(bl) U.S. Environmental Protection Agency(bm) Seymour Chwast(br) 116–119 ©Jaqui Wong 128 Renee Lynn/Photo Researchers, Inc.(b) **Theme 4:** 135 Susan Van Etten/Stock Boston(br) 137 The Granger Collection(b) 138 Stock Montage, Inc.(tl) Brown Brothers(tr) 139 Brown Brothers(t) 139 Culver Pictures, Inc.(m) 140 Culver Pictures, Inc.(tl) The Boeing Company Archives(tr) The Bettmann Archive(b) 141 Tony Freeman/Photo Edit(tl) The Boeing Company Archives(tr) Dean Siracusa/FPG International(bl) NASA(br) 144 Brown Brothers(b) Courtesy of Pierre D. Boy(t) 145 Courtesy of Jean B. Murdoch(t) Jon Reis/The Stock Market(tr) 146 Courtesy of Mrs. Verdugo(l) 154 The Bettmann Archive 155 Bill Losh/FPG International(t) 156 John Buitenkant/Photo Researchers(tl) C. Navaswan/FPG(br) 157 Joseph Nettis/Photo Researchers(bl) Blair Seitz/Photo Researchers(br) **Big Book Theme 5** inside front cover The Granger Collection 1 David James/Tony Stone Images/Chicago, Inc.(b) 19 Photri/The Stock Market 24–25 David A. Hardy/Science Photo Library 25 Earth Imaging/Tony Stone Images/Chicago, Inc.(m) 26 Verna Johnson/Photo Researchers, Inc.(background) **Glossary:** 180 Tom Pix/Peter Arnold Inc.(tl) Mark Richards/Photo Editlm) David J. Boyle/Animals Animals/Earth Scenes(bl) Barrie Rokeach 1981(trm) Stephen Marks/Stockphotos(brm) Mug Shots/The Stock Market(br) Jean Wisenbaugh ©1995 181 Gary Gladstone/Image Bank(tl) Steve Dunwell/Image Bank(tlm) Icon Communications/FPG International(cl) Peter French/Bruce Coleman Inc.(blm) Jose L. Pelarez/The Stock Market(bl) Jim Nilsen/Tony Stone Images(tr) Murray Alcosser/Image Bank(trm) Myrleen Ferguson/Photo Edit(brm) Don Klumpp/Image Bank(br) 182 Michael Heron/The Stock Market(tl) Don Carl Steffen/Photo Researchers(tlm) Bob Daemmrich/Stock Boston(cl) Eddie Hironaka/Image Bank(blm) Jay Freis/Image Bank(bl) Bob Daemmrich/Stock Boston(tr) Library of Congress(trm) JC Carton/Bruce Coleman Inc.(cr) Joe Devenney/Image Bank(brm) Bob Daemmrich/Image Works(br) 183 Craig Aurness/Westlight(tl) Peter Hendrie/Image Bank(tlm) Goodwood Productions/Image Bank(bl) Alan Becker/Image Bank(tr) Peter Vanderwarker/Stock Boston(br) **Atlas Glossary:** 27 Eddie Hironaka/Image Bank(ml) Henryk T. Kaiser/Picture Cube, Inc.(bl) Chris Hackett/Image Bank(tr) Bernard Roussel/Image Bank(mr) R. P. Kingston/Picture Cube, Inc.(cr) Earth Imaging/Tony Stone Images/Chicago, Inc.(brm) William Edward Smith/The Stock Market(br)